Barbara Katagiri

"Why don't we have a sexy Yakuza who never thought of being pushed down by a man—be caught and forced to use his body as payment?" I wrote, joking. To think this would be the story of my first Biblos novel...it's like opening a present. I'm really happy.

Illustrated By
Sakuya Fujii

Sleeping with Money
札束のベッドで眠れ

Written by
BARBARA KATAGIRI

Illustrations by
SAKUYA FUJII

English translation by
Translation By Design

June

Los Angeles

SLEEPING WITH MONEY

Written by Barbara Katagiri
Illustrated by Sakuya Fujii
English translation by Translation By Design

English Edition Published by:
DIGITAL MANGA PUBLISHING
A division of DIGITAL MANGA, Inc.
1487 W 178th Street, Suite 300
Gardena, CA 90248
USA
www.dmpbooks.com
www.junemanga.com

Library of Congress Cataloging-in-Publication Data Available Upon Request

First Edition: June 2008
ISBN-13: 978-1-56970-738-8
10 9 8 7 6 5 4 3 2 1

Printed in China

Other novels published by
JUNÉ

Only The Ring Finger Knows vol.1
The Lonely Ring Finger

Don't Worry Mama

The Man Who Doesn't
Take Off His Clothes vol.1-2

Cold Sleep

Little Darling

Ai No Kusabi – The Space Between
Vol.1- Stranger

Sweet Admiration

Caged Slave

Contents

You Gotta Be Kidding!

Mounted atop Tatsurou Yamamoto, Yoshiaki Sagami whispered in his soft coaxing voice, "Are you ready?"

Tatsurou's wrists were tied up and secured to the headboard. It didn't matter how ready he was, he would never get over the humiliation of being tied down by another man. He was breaking out into a cold sweat and things hadn't even started yet.

Idiot! he screamed inside as he glared at Sagami. *This is bullshit! I'm a Yakuza! A Yakuza boss. When I walk down the street, people leap out of my way!*

He had eyes like a ravenous beast's, a long slender nose, and thin lips. His body wasn't all that muscular, but his physique was as smooth as a drawn sword. He still couldn't understand why another man would covet his body.

"N-n-n-no, I'm not!" he yelled.

He pushed Sagami back and tried to stand up. But with his hands tied and Sagami's more powerful body mounted on top of him, Tatsurou couldn't move an inch. He was a sitting duck, plain and simple.

"Come on, behave yourself. I'll be gentle." Sagami pushed down Tatsurou's jaw with his finger and spoke to him like a child.

Sagami had an unusual mix of facial features.

His face was a strange balance of wildness and nobility; masculine, yet delicate. His features had managed to captivate even Tatsurou when they had first met.

Sagami fixed an irreverent gaze on Tatsurou, then skillfully unbuttoned his shirt with one hand.

"Get off me, you bastard!" Tatsurou screamed as Sagami's hand touched his bare skin.

He struggled with all his might to throw off Sagami, but Sagami didn't budge. Tatsurou only managed to kick up his knees. He had no effective means of resistance left.

Bastard!

"You're a lively one," Sagami said. "I'm liking you more and more."

His breath tickled Tatsurou's neck. The tip of his tongue slithered across Tatsurou's jaw, giving the helpless man goosebumps. Tatsurou felt weak and powerless.

"No!" he yelled again.

Despite his desperate struggling, Tatsurou couldn't change the situation he was in. To make matters worse, Sagami's lips had found his own.

"Ngh…no…ah…" he mumbled.

He tried to bite down, but Sagami's finger firmly held his jaw in place. Sagami must have known he would try to bite him.

Their lips locked. Tatsurou found it hard to draw breath. He could feel a bead of saliva slowly drip from the corner of his mouth.

This can't be happening, he thought.

Ever since he had participated in the sake-sharing ceremony, the initiation ritual of the Kantou Hinodegumi, he had been treated with respect. Yet this man wasn't scared of him, and even dared to subject him to this.

Bastard! You bastard! Get off of me!

Once Tatsurou might have agreed to this, but now he was screaming for Sagami to stop. The most embarrassing part was that he was powerless to resist.

"Ngh."

Each time Sagami's tongue moved in his mouth, Tatsurou felt more and more confused. He shivered and he was dripping with sweat. He was beginning to understand what it must feel like to be a girl. The little shockwaves of passion that he felt whenever Sagami's tongue moved seemed all too enjoyable.

Get off me!

Disturbed by his own feelings, Tatsurou closed his eyes and recalled the chain of events that had brought him here.

Tatsurou worked as a lower-level boss for the Kantou Hinodegumi, a small gang that operated in the Ueno district of Tokyo.

Unlike in the past, present-day Yakuza managed respectable businesses, participated in finance and land speculations, and even played the stock market. But the violent Hinodegumi gang was different. Even if they wanted to fight, they had no real opponents. The police were cracking down on them more and more each day.

To make matters worse, their numbers were

decreasing. That was why Tatsurou had managed to climb up the ladder while he was still in his 20s.

The Hinodegumi couldn't find a good way of making money these days. Lately, their main source of revenue was collecting bad loans for a financial company called "Lovely."

"G-good morning! Boss!" Hachi said with a deep bow as Tatsurou entered the office.

"Yo," Tatsurou grunted. He quickly nodded and headed for his desk.

Hachi was Tatsurou's foolish assistant. He was tall, gangly and clumsy, but his face was full of youth, like a naughty teenager's. You might say that he was cute in a way, but he spent most of his free time admiring himself in the mirror. Whenever he went to eat lunch, he would get in a bad mood after he finished, then pick a fight with the chef to avoid paying. This was partly because he was stingy, but mostly because he didn't earn enough money to actually pay.

Tatsurou noticed Hachi was looking gloomily at him and raised an eyebrow.

"What?" he asked.

To his surprise, Hachi's shoulders were shaking and his cheeks were bright pink. He looked as if he had just awakened from a dream.

"I'm not a proud man," Hachi said, "but I *am* a real ladies' man."

"Hmm," Tatsurou said noncommittally.

"Men are usually out of the question for me. But I can't keep it in anymore." Hachi suddenly exploded. "I love you! When I see you my heart goes—"

Tatsurou gave Hachi a swift kick.

Yes, Tatsurou was slim and attractive for a Yakuza. Some people joked that he should be a gigolo, but few men could match his physical strength. Anyone who didn't show him the respect he deserved was asking to get beat up.

He calmly took a fax from Lovely off the table. Lovely had a very wholesome public image, mostly because of their cute TV commercial that featured kittens. But whenever they couldn't collect a debt, they called in the Yakuza.

Tatsurou took the cup of tea that Hachi offered and picked up the phone.

"Hello, are you Satou? My name is Yamamoto. Did you borrow money from Lovely?" he asked in a low voice tinged with menace.

He didn't mention who sent him. He didn't want people to alert the authorities. But the tone of his voice definitely cried Yakuza. He heard Satou swallow nervously.

This tactic would probably be enough to finish the job. Most people immediately gave in when they got a call from the Yakuza. Even so, Tatsurou pushed on, making sure he'd only have to make one call.

"Looks like you've been having some problems. How about you pay it back without any more excuses?" he said in a softer tone.

Satou breathed a sigh of relief.

"I can't pay now. But I can at the end of the month," he promised.

"Hmm. Interesting proposition, Mr. Satou,"

Tatsurou said coldly. Then he bellowed from the pit of his stomach, "Don't give me excuses! PAY UP! Your home, your business, your wife and children, your relatives—I know all about them! If you don't pay up soon, we'll be paying *you* a visit!"

There was a squeak on the other end, then Satou promised to pay sooner. Tatsurou made a note and hung up the phone.

Enough of this petty work, he thought. He turned to Hachi.

"That's how you do it," he said. "You do the rest."

He passed the list to Hachi, propped his legs up on the desk, and took out a cigarette. Hachi immediately jumped up to light it for him. Tatsurou stretched out and took a drag. He was in charge of this office, but few people worked here.

The phone rang.

Tatsurou instantly picked up the receiver, since Hachi was in the middle of another call. He needed another person to man the phones, but had no money to hire more people.

"Kantou Hinodegumi!" he yelled into the phone. Once, at the very beginning of his career, his boss had smashed an ashtray over his head for being too soft on the phone. That man no longer worked there, either.

"Tatsurou? It's me," the voice on the other line said.

As soon as he heard the man's voice, Tatsurou took his feet off his desk. It was the president of the Kantou Hinodegumi, calling from the main office.

"Sir," he snapped out.

"Come here now," the president said. "We've found a real gold mine."

That was the beginning of it all.

The job from the president regarded a delinquent promissory note.

Tatsurou drove down the bank alongside the backstreet factory in a Benz S-Class. Though he had no money, he still wore a fine Italian-made suit, so people would instantly recognize him as a Yakuza.

He got out of the car and put a cigarette between his lips. Hachi again offered a light. Taking a puff, Tatsurou surveyed the factory.

Hmph.

He was in a foul mood. He never thought he'd have to come back here like this. His vision clouded by tobacco smoke, he looked around feeling a little sick inside.

I've just gotta forget it.

It was just an old car factory near a residential neighborhood. There was nothing special about it.

He strode towards the building looking cocky. When he got to the fence, he saw a big crowd of men.

"Outta the way!" he growled, stubbing his cigarette out with his shoe.

Just like what the Dead Sea had done for Moses, the crowd parted to let him through. They might have also been debt-collecting thugs, but Tatsurou was a real Yakuza, a step-up from them. He kicked open the door and stepped inside.

The factory was spacious, but he didn't see any employees. He looked around, hoping to spot something of value.

"Argh!" he suddenly cried out as freezing cold water splashed over his head. Getting soaked to the skin on a chilly October day was more than a little unpleasant.

"GET OUT!" yelled an old man in a uniform.

Tatsurou squinted at him. He didn't expect to see *him* here.

It's you.

"I'm gonna get you!" Hachi snarled, lunging at the old man.

"Hachi, stop!" Tatsurou commanded.

Hachi instantly did as told.

"We're not here to pick fights," Tatsurou warned. "He'll go to the police and make trouble. Then we won't get what we came here for."

He pushed back his wet hair. Water dripped from the edge of his sleeve.

"Are you Mr. Uchida?" he asked, not making eye contact. He had avoided this place for such a long time. What would Uchida do when he realized that Tatsurou was Yakuza? But Uchida was less cooperative than expected.

"Get out!" the old man howled.

That scream was his only reaction. Tatsurou's mouth twisted. The only one here who cared that Tatsurou was Yakuza was Tatsurou himself. As far as Uchida was concerned, Yakuza were on the same level as dog shit.

No matter. That would just make it easier for Tatsurou.

He snorted and glared at Uchida.

"Stop messing around. Let's be adult about this," he ordered, folding his arms across his drenched suit.

Uchida picked up the bucket and started refilling it with water.

"Hey, wait!" Tatsurou pleaded.

Uchida threw the bucket at him again.

This time the water felt even colder.

"Dammit!" Tatsurou cursed as he left the factory.

He was the only one who got wet. Lucky Hachi didn't get a drop on him.

As Tatsurou glared, the crowd at the entrance quickly made way for him.

He walked towards the Benz. His entire body was wet. This was not something a Yakuza could let pass.

"Are you all right? Please dry yourself, boss. You'll catch a cold," Hachi pleaded, handing him a towel.

Tatsurou wiped the water from his hair, which now looked like seaweed, then blotted his wet suit. He was soaked through to his underwear.

Hachi watched Tatsurou with fascination, his cheeks turning pink.

"Boss," he began.

"Hmm?" Tatsurou said, still trying to dry himself off.

"You're such a great guy," Hachi continued. "Even while soaked from head to toe, no one could look as good as you do."

Though it was supposed to be a compliment, it felt a little creepy. Hachi's intense gaze made Tatsurou feel a little queasy.

"Shut the fuck up," he grunted, hitting Hachi over the head. As he peeled off his dripping suit, cold air cut through his wet shirt.

"Ugh, it's cold," he muttered.

Rubbing his sore head, Hachi glanced at Tatsurou. "Uh, this is kinda hard to ask, boss," he said.

"What?" Tatsurou growled.

"Can you leave the shirt on? You're kinda turning me on," Hachi mumbled.

"Huh?" Tatsurou sputtered, then gave Hachi a sharp kick.

"Ooof!" Hachi groaned, rolling on the ground in agony.

Tatsurou climbed into the driver's seat and set the heat on high. He couldn't think about Hachi right now. His head was full of thoughts of Uchida.

What's his problem? he wondered, resting his elbows on the steering wheel.

He really thought he could do this. He hadn't been in that place for so long. He figured he could just collect the money and feel no pain. But seeing Uchida's face brought back all the old memories.

Ten long years ago. The days when young

Tatsurou spent his time caught up in gang violence.

"That's why. I have duties and obligations, too,"
Tatsurou mumbled drunkenly to a stranger at the bar.

He'd gone home to change and then headed out
to the town. By now, he'd tossed back enough drinks that
he barely knew where he was. He just needed someone
to listen to him. Now he was telling this stranger his life
story.

"Being a Yakuza means cutting ties with
your real family," he went on. "It's really for the best.
Otherwise, you'd first fuck over your brothers. Then
you'd fuck over your friends. You'd take all their money
and chew them down to their bones. That's what it's
like to be Yakuza. Hey, are you listening to me? You
bastard!"

The man next to him stayed calm. "I'm
listening," he said. "So you cut yourself off, huh?"

Tatsurou smiled and poured the glass of brandy
down his throat. No longer able to sit upright, he rested
his head on the bar and continued to talk.

"I didn't really have anyone to cut ties with. I
had already left home. When I went back, some stranger
was living there instead of my family. Guess my old
lady hooked up with some boyfriend and took off.
My old man wasn't around either. Money troubles or
something."

He screwed up his face. It had been a dark time,
a past he didn't care to remember.

"He owed something like a million yen. No way

could a kid pay that back. I tried to ignore the Yakuza who came to collect, but they just beat me up. Later they took me to their office. And from then on, their boss was my new dad. Only one other person tried to help me."

"Really? Who was that?" the stranger asked calmly.

He sounded like he came from a better class of people. Tatsurou was delighted to have such a patient listener. It felt cathartic to spill his guts this way.

"When I was messing around in the streets, I used to fight at the dry river bed. I probably fought several hundred people," Tatsurou continued.

True, he had been in a gang during school. But no way was that number correct. It was probably more like 20 people, but Tatsurou loved to embellish the facts.

"Once we wound up facing a huge crowd. These guys just wanted to beat the shit out of us. I ran into some factory while covered in blood. I tried to hide, but this old guy saw me. The rival gang was beating on the shutters, yelling for me to come out. I was stuck between a rock and a hard place. I thought they'd burst in any second and beat me half to death, or even kill me. I figured I was a goner. In those days, it was kill or be killed. But the old man offered me a job if I left my gang. Promised to help me."

Tatsurou had always remembered the old man's words.

"He said I reminded him of his son. 'Is he a bad ass like me?' I asked. Then he dragged me to the family altar. His son had died in an accident. The old man looked at me with tears in his eyes. 'Do you want me to chase you outside? Or will you become an honest man?'"

"So? What did you choose?" the stranger asked.

Tatsurou rubbed his chin on the bar.

"I'd been beat up pretty badly," he said. "And I didn't wanna die like a loser. So I started wondering if I should get a real job. I actually felt kinda happy. It was the first time someone had ever said stuff like that to me and actually meant it. That stubborn old man. So, yeah, I made him a promise. He chased away the thugs who were banging on the shutters and looked after me."

"Sounds like you broke your promise," the stranger said in a teasing voice.

Even in his drunken state, Tatsurou noticed and looked up. Yakuza hated being made fun of more than anything. Disrespect isn't good for business.

"Shut up! I said I had a debt to pay!" he growled.

He suddenly looked around. He was in an unfamiliar, high-class club, sitting at one end of the dark stone bar. It was a small place, only four tables and a bar. The hostesses didn't even approach the two men.

He turned to squint at the stranger, who was still relaxing next to him. The stranger, who had a noble-looking nose, was an attractive man that even a man could fall for.

Have I met him before?

The stranger wore a fine British-made suit, different from typical Yakuza wear. His legs were crossed in an ostentatious way.

The man calmly returned Tatsurou's gaze. He didn't seem to be at all afraid of Yakuza, which made Tatsurou mad.

"You don't look like an honest man," the man commented.

The alcohol had made Tatsurou volatile.

"Are you making fun of me?!" he screamed. He grabbed the man's head and was about to slam it on the bar when an arm reached out to stop him.

What?

Now he recognized the man's face. Only one person had ever been better than him. Only one person had ever made him taste bitter defeat. Only one person had beaten him in the regional school finals, 10 long years ago.

As soon as he realized who it was, Tatsurou felt acid rise from the pit of his stomach.

"You're Yoshiaki Sagami!" he yelled.

Sagami calmly lifted his whisky glass to his lips and took a slow sip, glancing seductively at Tatsurou.

"Yep," he said. "Been a long time, Tatsurou. But when we met at Uchida's you totally ignored me."

"Uchida's?" Tatsurou echoed.

Did Uchida owe money to Sagami, too?

"After all these years, you still look at me with such complete disgust. I feel hurt," Sagami went on.

"Huh, what are you saying?! You bastard!" Tatsurou snarled.

They had always talked to each other like this, from the very first moment they'd met. Now Sagami seemed to be enjoying Tatsurou's foul mood.

"Glad I came back to Japan because I got to see you again, Tatsurou," Sagami said. "I still dream about your eyes. Meeting you again like this, after so long. Is it a gift from the heavens or the whim of the gods?"

"Hah?!" Tatsurou croaked, looking suspiciously at Sagami.

They hadn't seen each other since high school graduation. After that, Tatsurou had never known, nor even cared, where Sagami was.

Now he was trying to crack Sagami's skull open. It was a fitting reunion, at least. But when Tatsurou tried to stand up, his knees gave out from under him. He let Sagami put him back on the stool, all the while telling himself this jerk would be running home to mommy right now. If only he wasn't drunk, that is.

"You okay?" Sagami asked, his hands still around Tatsurou's waist. "Your body's as fit as ever."

Tatsurou felt uneasy. It wasn't right for a man to touch him like that.

Sagami kept on smiling. Tatsurou wondered how he could be so calm in the presence of a Yakuza.

Bastard!

During their school days, Sagami was Tatsurou's Kendo rival, but they had only met at regional competitions. Tatsurou went to a bad school, while Sagami attended a top prep academy, guaranteed to get him into a good university. Tatsurou had instantly hated the excellent students and their privileged upbringings.

Why couldn't I beat this guy?

Thinking back, Tatsurou recalled his anger as

if it had been yesterday.

Sagami returned Tatsurou's glare with an inviting smile, like one you might give a girl you were interested in.

What the hell is this guy thinking?

Just as Tatsurou was about to unleash another round of expletives, Sagami started to talk.

"I don't mind you looking at me like that. But continue your story if you want. I'm interested. I can tell just by looking that you didn't become an honest man. What happened to your promise to Uchida?"

He looked eager to hear more, but Tatsurou cut the conversation short with a sullen look and a curt reply. "Nothing happened."

Sagami looked confused. "Huh?"

"That's it," Tatsurou said. "My body got better, and so did my mind. I forgot all about my promise to that old man."

The truth was he would never forget Uchida's parting words:

"If you ever have no place to go, you can always come to me. I'll train you."

Today he went to Uchida's factory.

Tatsurou had no home and no family, so the factory had been somewhere he could always go to, an emotional means of support. Whatever happened, whatever he lost, at least he had a place that would always welcome him, no questions asked. Knowing that, he had felt he could do anything. And he kept on believing that, even after he started his Yakuza life.

But, truth be told, the honest part of his life

had been just an illusion. As he dove deeper and deeper into the underground world, his soul became dirtier and dirtier. Before he knew it, he had stopped going to Uchida's factory. Respectable people lived there. It was no longer a haven for him.

Uchida had completely forgotten about Tatsurou. That should have been a relief, but instead he was annoyed. It really pissed him off. He couldn't help but feel lonely, like the world had rejected him. Something was still left in his heart.

"So you felt sad and turned to the bottle, huh? It won't help you, but it's kinda cute," Sagami said.

"Huh? I never said I was depressed!" Tatsurou protested.

"That's what you wanted to say, though," Sagami retorted. "You're drunk and emotional, just longing for someone to listen to you."

Not mocking him anymore, Sagami poured some expensive Hennessey into Tatsurou's glass in an attempt to humor him.

Sagami was definitely making him mad. But the alcohol was free, and it'd be a shame to waste it.

Tatsurou chugged down his glass. The warm liquid burned his belly. He felt his consciousness slipping even further away.

"So what did you do?" Sagami prompted. "Finish the story. What will you do about the collection?"

Sagami's voice sounded far away. Though the world was furiously spinning around him, he still wanted to talk. And as if the alcohol was a truth serum, Tatsurou obediently answered.

"I can't tell the president I couldn't get it. The big shots expect us to obey. You can't get caught up in your own feelings, or they'll chop off a finger."

"A finger?" Sagami echoed.

Tatsurou held up his hands. He still had all his fingers. And he didn't have a tattoo. Still, going against a Yakuza boss was not a good idea. He had already been beaten up a number of times.

Sagami smiled down at him. "So why don't you leave? I'll help you out. Do you have the note for Uchida's place?"

Tatsurou pulled out the promissory note from his pocket. He hated to betray someone who had helped him. If there was any way out of this mess, he wanted to hear it.

Sagami instantly touched his lighter to the note as Tatsurou held it. Tatsurou watched with astonishment as the paper caught fire.

Huuuuh?

Finally wrenched out of his dream-like state, Tatsurou gaped at his burning fingers.

"OUCH!" he yelled. He'd let go of the note just a second too late. It quickly turned to ashes.

"There you go," Sagami said. "All gone now. Here, drink."

While Tatsurou looked bewildered, Sagami just laughed and shrugged his shoulders. Tatsurou felt himself melt when he gazed at Sagami's profile, but that handsome face couldn't deceive him.

Dammit! That was worth six million. Without it, they wouldn't get a single penny.

Tatsurou felt like screaming, but Sagami chuckled again. His laugh must have been contagious for Tatsurou also started to cackle.

It's gone.

One simple act had completely wiped out his problem. It was so weird. He couldn't stop laughing like an idiot.

That was the last thing he remembered from that night.

"Urrrghh," Tatsurou groaned. He was sprawled on the sofa, his head pounding. He had been throwing up all night. Finally, it was morning.

Hachi was now cleaning up the mess. The boy had even opened the curtains.

"Hachi," Tatsurou muttered, squinting.

"What is it, boss?"

"Get me some Tylenol."

Changing positions made him feel even worse. Why did he drink so much?

He rolled up his sleeves and started thinking about last night. Maybe it had all been just a dream. Meeting his old high school rival. Burning the valuable promissory note.

It was a dream. It had to be a dream.

What a nightmare. He just had to stop drinking so much. He dug into his pockets. He was still wearing yesterday's suit, so the note should still be there.

But it wasn't.

In a panic, he pulled all of his pockets inside

out, but he still found nothing. Just then, he felt a twinge from his burned fingertips.

It wasn't a dream!

Tatsurou's mind blanked out in despair. Hachi shook his shoulders, bringing him back to reality.

"Hey, stop that!" he barked, glaring at Hachi.

Hachi passed him the cordless phone.

"It's the president," he whispered.

Tatsurou instantly came to attention—and felt an overwhelming desire to puke. He sat up as straight as he could and put the phone to his ear.

"Ah, how was it? Did it go well?" the president asked immediately.

Tatsurou broke out in a cold sweat. Did the president already know about the burned note?

"Ah, yes, that. I'm, uh, getting there," he replied meekly.

Why was the president calling so soon? He'd given the job to Tatsurou just yesterday.

"You have until the day after tomorrow," the president said gravely.

"Huh?" Tatsurou replied blankly.

"Don't speak to me like that, Tatsurou," the president said. "You have the note. I want that six million the day after tomorrow. Make that ten million, for all the hassle. I expect cash, okay?"

Ten million?

Tatsurou knew right off that that would be impossible. No way could he pull that off. But he couldn't tell the president that. His hangover quickly disappeared as he desperately considered what to do next. He was dripping with sweat, though his mouth was bone dry.

"Uh, sir, we checked out the factory yesterday," he frantically said. "Found nothing of value, just scrap iron, tools, and a worn out old man."

"He has land, though, so no excuses," the president replied. "Make him sign over the deeds. Ignore anyone who says there's a repossession order. We need to sell the land for ten million."

"B-but the old man is stubborn," Tatsurou insisted. "I don't think he'll sign—"

He had never thought to ask Uchida to simply sell the land. Even if he still had the promissory note, convincing the old man would not be easy. Now that the note was history, it was completely out of the question. He was at even less of an advantage than before.

"If you can't do it, bring me the note now," the president said crisply. "You're useless. I'll send someone else. I want that ten million the day after tomorrow. It better happen. You have the note, just force the old man. Make him sign. It's simple enough."

Tatsurou didn't dare tell him what had happened to the note. But what else could he do? He sadly curled his fingers. Which one of them would he lose?

His mind went completely blank. If another gang member took over, who knew what they would do to Uchida. He couldn't risk the old man's safety. Even his shaky morals wouldn't allow it.

"Uh, no problem. It's, uh, fine. Leave it to me. I'll have the ten million the day after tomorrow," he managed to say, though his face looked deathly pale.

The president laughed, satisfied. "Good! I'm relying on you, Tatsurou. Don't let me down."

"Sir."

Tatsurou hung up, but still gripped the phone. He couldn't move. It was now or never time. He'd been given his orders.

Ten million in two days?

He felt more cold sweat dripping down his back.

Getting money from Uchida without a note would be even harder. If the old man contacted the police, that would be it.

That bastard!

"Hachi! Do you know how to make money?" Tatsurou groaned.

"I do," Hachi said calmly, handing over the Tylenol.

"How do you do it?" Tatsurou asked.

"Used girls' panties are a great source of income," Hachi replied. "I buy cheap panties, wear them myself, then sell them on the Internet with some good pictures. You can make three million in a month. Wanna try it, sir?"

Tatsurou eyed Hachi with suspicion. Hachi had been flashing cash around recently. Tatsurou had definitely wondered where it came from, but never thought Hachi would stoop *that* low.

"With your resources, you could really get it going," Hachi said excitedly.

Tatsurou whacked him over the head. Hachi sank to the floor and crawled out of the office.

First things first. Tatsurou needed to find the jerk who had burned the note. Sagami looked like someone with some cash. Maybe not a full ten million, but Tatsurou could at least get the six back. Seeing Sagami again didn't exactly thrill him, though. He racked his brains, trying to remember the bar from last night.

He glanced at his watch. It was still early. He decided to collect money elsewhere until the bars opened.

"I found you, bastard! Think I'd let you get away with that?" Tatsurou yelled. When he had finally found the bar, Sagami was sitting there, just as he'd hoped.

He stormed inside, itching to start a fight. The group of girls hovering around Sagami took one look at Tatsurou and fled. Tatsurou lunged at Sagami, who deftly dodged away.

Huh?

Tatsurou looked down at his arm, which had again been stopped in midair. He had forgotten all about last night. His desire to punch Sagami's lights out was not entirely due to alcohol.

"Pretty popular with the ladies, eh?" he sneered. "No surprise, I guess. You are rich, young, and handsome."

He was trying to distract Sagami, but the man calmly nodded.

"Thanks. Take a seat, Tatsurou."

Sagami looked like a millionaire. Feeling the man's fierce sexual energy, Tatsurou crashed down on the stool next to him. He leaned back with his arms crossed, spread his legs wide, and glowered at Sagami.

"You know what happened yesterday," he growled. "How are you gonna fix things?"

"Fix things?" Sagami echoed.

"You burned my note," Tatsurou hissed. "The six million. That was as good as money. You'd better fucking pay it back, with some interest added for my time."

Making threats. Raising issues over the amount. Getting aggressive. This was how the Yakuza operated.

But Sagami's reply was amazingly calm. "No."

"WHAT?" Tatsurou howled.

"No. It was dishonored. It was totally worthless. It can't be used or considered as money," Sagami said firmly, perfectly clear about where he stood on the matter.

It infuriated Tatsurou that Sagami wasn't the least bit intimidated by him. So he lost it.

"Hey, pretty boy! Outside, now!" he jeered, kicking over a table and lunging at the man's neck again.

Sagami easily evaded him, then grabbed his tie and pulled him closer.

"Let's talk about this reasonably, Tatsurou," he gently cooed.

Tatsurou noticed a sadistic glint in Sagami's eyes—and choked. Who the hell was this guy?

"Ba-bastard!" he yelled.

He knew every gang around here. But he'd never seen Sagami among them. The man looked honest, but he was definitely not an ordinary guy.

Sagami pushed Tatsurou away and pointed to a quiet area.

"Let's talk back there," he said. "Then we won't disturb the other customers."

"If you insist," Tatsurou muttered, trying to look tough.

Sagami stood up. He was a good head taller than Tatsurou. Tatsurou shivered a little, remembering how tough Sagami had been during competition.

They settled down in the back of the room. After a hostess brought them drinks and snacks, they were left looking at each other. Tatsurou got right down to business.

"Pay up," he growled.

"Why?" Sagami said coolly.

He looked like he was enjoying himself, and poured more sake into Tatsurou's glass.

"Don't give me this shit," Tatsurou said. "Pay up *now!*"

"If you need money, then sell your car," Sagami suggested. "A Benz S-Class should fetch a decent price."

How does he know what I drive?

Tatsurou raised an eyebrow. When did he start talking to him last night? He had been too drunk to remember. He decided to tell the truth, hoping to get Sagami's sympathy.

"It's not mine," he admitted.

"Huh?"

"My gang's dirt poor," Tatsurou explained

further. "It's not my car. I'm borrowing it. If I sold it, God knows what would happen to me."

"Huh? Not in a good financial position then?" Sagami said.

"Shut up," Tatsurou snapped.

He was getting tired of this game. Sagami could care less that he was a Yakuza.

Tatsurou sulked and lit a cigarette. Sagami's eyes oozed sexual attraction. Tatsurou was even more irritated that the other man was using that power on him.

"Tatsurou," Sagami said.

"Yeah?"

Sagami moved closer to Tatsurou, who instantly froze. Suddenly Sagami touched his thigh.

"Do you like being a Yakuza, even though nobody cares anymore?" Sagami asked.

Tatsurou gasped and quickly moved away.

What the fuck is wrong with this guy?

But secretly, he understood. Tatsurou himself was more interested in men's legs, too.

Suddenly he knew why this guy bothered him so much. If he played it up now, maybe Sagami wouldn't laugh it off so easily.

He let out a creepy laugh. "It's fun. Beating up another person, arguing, the intense moments. So exciting. Your head goes blank, and the ecstasy is almost as good as an orgasm."

He really wanted a good showdown now.

Sagami must have sensed it, but he didn't flinch and spoke calmly. "Yes, I know what you mean. When you glare at me like that, I feel little shivers, too. How can I get a man like you to have me?"

Tatsurou didn't understand him for a minute.

"Huh?" he croaked.

But when he grasped what Sagami was saying, he went ballistic. How dare he mock him! Tatsurou glared at Sagami, his almond eyes gleaming with pure hatred.

"Stop mocking me!" he yelled. "Just pay me! I need ten million! It's all your fault for burning that note!"

He didn't expect screaming would do any good.

Sagami just shrugged his shoulders, a habit he must have picked up from dealing with foreigners. "But you said it had been dishonored," he said. "You couldn't get any money from it. We'll have to settle in court. I can recommend a good lawyer."

Sagami knew what he was talking about. But for good or for bad, extracting money was a Yakuza's job. They couldn't let themselves be talked down.

"You'd better take responsibility!" Tatsurou insisted. "If I can't get the money out of that old man, *you'll* have to pay!"

"I said no," Sagami said.

"Bullshit! If I tell you to pay, then you damn well better pay. I need ten million by tomorrow," Tatsurou screamed.

"Why do you need money that bad?" Sagami asked.

"Shut up," Tatsurou said.

"I just have to get it, somehow."

"Somehow?" Sagami's eyes sparkled. He smiled like a little kid about to pull a prank.

Now Tatsurou grabbed Sagami's tie and pulled tight. This time he would make things crystal clear.

"Come with me," he said. "You did this and you're gonna end it. I'll make sure of that."

"Good," Sagami agreed almost gleefully. "Let's go."

He still wasn't perturbed in the least. Even after Tatsurou decided that they would go to Uchida's together.

At the factory, Tatsurou and Sagami were greeted by another water hose.

"Don't come here again! I have no money to give maggots like you!" Uchida snapped.

Tatsurou wanted to yell back, but a cop car was parked nearby. Shady loan sharks were a real problem in this part of town.

Yakuza always avoided the police as much as possible. They would have to try to collect again later that night, when the cops were not around.

When they left the factory, it was even colder outside than it was yesterday. They both felt chilled to the bone. Tatsurou's teeth chattered. Sagami had gotten doused, too, leaving little puddles of water in his wake.

"Maggots!" Tatsurou snarled.

Sagami laughed at him, looking like a happy boy who'd just been swimming.

"He was talking to you, too!" Tatsurou screamed as they reached the street where he'd parked the Benz. He had a change of clothes inside. But when he got there, his car had been towed away, replaced by a telephone number written on the road in chalk.

Don't give me this shit, Tatsurou thought, sick with rage and frustration.

He kicked the wall and stormed off, teeth still chattering. Even if he tried to flag a taxi to get home, no driver would pick up a wet Yakuza rat. They'd be afraid to get caught up in something dangerous.

"Hmph. Yakuza have it pretty rough, huh?"

Sagami was following him down the sidewalk. He'd whispered those words, sounding almost impressed.

"Just shut the fuck up," Tatsurou snarled. "This is all your goddamn fault."

"So! What are you gonna do now?" Sagami asked.

"What?" Tatsurou questioned back.

Sagami checked his Rolex. "You told me this was all my fault. Are you gonna leave me now? You need ten million by the day after tomorrow. It's 11:00 p.m. now. One day left. Got any ideas?"

"If I don't, will you lend me the money?" Tatsurou said, looking surly. Nothing was going right. Another taxi passed him by.

"You could try a loan shark," Sagami said.

How did Sagami know about that?

"Already did," Tatsurou told him. "All I could get was two million."

He'd spent the entire day looking for money. Now the cold and his frustration released themselves in a long, drawn-out sigh. He lost all desire to pretend. He was convinced that nobody understood how broke and how miserable a Yakuza could actually be.

I can't do this.

No way could he get the money now. Nowadays, Yakuza needed more than muscle, they needed business-savvy. Tatsurou had the muscle but not the business sense. In this modern world, physical strength was simply obsolete.

He sneezed. He had no hope. He just wanted to disappear.

"Wow. Usually you're so cheerful. Right now you look like a lost puppy," Sagami commented.

"Just shut the fuck up," Tatsurou said.

Sagami was as persistent as ever. Tatsurou raised an eyebrow. Did nothing intimidate this guy?

"Wanna come to my place? We can walk there from here. You can take a bath and I'll lend you some clothes," Sagami suggested.

"Who the hell wants your help?" Tatsurou grouched.

He pulled out his cell phone to call Hachi, but the stupid thing was waterlogged and wouldn't work.

"No use?" Sagami said dryly.

Frustrated yet again, Tatsurou threw the phone to the ground.

Would this living hell never stop?

Despite all this, Sagami was still smiling.

"Come on. You'll catch a cold," he said kindly,

grabbing Tatsurou's wrist to pull him along.

"Let go of me," Tatsurou protested.

He pulled away, but Sagami continued walking, leaving him behind. The man almost looked like he enjoyed being soaked clear through.

Why him?

Tatsurou glared at Sagami's back, but could feel his rage subsiding.

It was strange.

Why wasn't Sagami scared of him? What could Tatsurou do to someone he didn't understand?

And then…

He didn't even know why he followed Sagami.

Because it's cold.

That was the excuse he told himself.

No taxi would stop, and his cell was D.O.A. He sneezed again and turned the corner. Sagami waited at the crosswalk and pulled something from his pocket.

"I forgot to give you my business card," he said, holding out a card that was damp around the edges.

Tatsurou looked down at it.

Lovely (Ltd) Kantou Assistant to the Branch Manager.

Lovely?

He'd been had.

"You work for Lovely?" Tatsurou frowned.

"My grandfather founded the company," Sagami admitted. "I'll be the third person to inherit it. I've been off training in New York. Finally got back to Japan last month."

"What?" Tatsurou muttered. He twitched nervously.

Now he knew why Sagami looked like money. Last year, Lovely had made the "top 10 richest companies" list. But behind closed doors, they had a secret business relationship with the Kantou Hinodegumi.

Of course, that didn't mean that Tatsurou would back down. He couldn't.

"If you need money, we can lend it to you," Sagami said, hurrying across the crosswalk.

"Huh?" Tatsurou blinked.

"Officially, we can't lend to crooks," Sagami said. "This will be a special case. We'd need some collateral, of course."

"Really?" Tatsurou squeaked. His voice had raised a whole octave at Sagami's offer to help. If he could just gather enough money now, he could sort it all out later. The knot in his stomach started to unravel.

"Really," Sagami assured him.

"But I don't have any collateral," Tatsurou said. "This will have to be a secret from the gang. I have no house. Even my car is borrowed."

"Your body is fine," Sagami said.

Tatsurou exited the crosswalk and stopped. He turned to see Sagami looking at him with piercing eyes.

"Your body will do fine, I said," Sagami repeated.

"Hah?" Tatsurou gaped at Sagami in astonishment. He couldn't form any other words.

Sagami wasn't joking. Tatsurou knew the offer was genuine.

"Sleep with me," Sagami said. "You said it,

remember? That you loved that moment of ecstasy where nothing matters. I think I could give you that."

"Fuck you!" Tatsurou snarled.

He hated being toyed with like this. He swiftly raised his knee to Sagami's crotch. Sagami blocked to avoid him, but Tatsurou swung back and kicked Sagami's face.

It hit cleanly this time.

Tatsurou wanted to hit him again, but his eyes caught the beam of a patrol car coming down the street.

He left Sagami and ran into the night.

Fucking jerk.

Tatsurou drank heavily until morning.

When Hachi woke him it was past noon. The president was calling again.

"Ah, Tatsurou. How's it going?" the president greeted.

Tatsurou couldn't tell him the truth—that he was nowhere near the ten million, and, in fact, had only managed two million.

"Well, getting there," Tatsurou mumbled.

"I see. Good," the president said, his voice softening a little. His own superiors were probably screaming at him, too.

"I'll have at least five million to you first thing tomorrow morning," Tatsurou promised.

He hung up the phone, then didn't move for five minutes.

Things get worse and worse...

He had always been really bad with money. He was also really bad at figuring out people's weak points. In so many ways, he was totally unsuited for this job.

What am I gonna do?

He sat up on the sofa. After two nights of hard drinking, his body felt like crap. How could he find more money today? His head felt ready to explode. He could never persuade anyone feeling like this.

"Hachi," he groaned.

"Yes, sir. Tylenol?" Hachi offered.

"How much money you got?" Tatsurou asked.

"About 8,000."

Suddenly, Hachi's three-million-a-month used panty business didn't seem quite so funny anymore. Tatsurou sighed. Taking money from Hachi would not make things better. He sprawled out on the sofa and soon fell asleep again. When he woke up, it was eight at night.

He had wasted the whole day, but it didn't really matter. He would have spent hours looking for money that just wasn't there. There was only one way to get out of this now.

I have to sell my body.

He let out a deep, deep sigh.

He'd rather sell his body than betray that old man again. He'd surely lose his pride, but maybe keep all of his fingers.

There was only one person who could give him enough money—the future president of Lovely.

When the phone call came from Tatsurou, Sagami smiled.

"Oh! What do you want with me today?" he said innocently, though he knew it was about the money. Tatsurou had kicked him last night, but Sagami definitely had planted a seed in Tatsurou's brain.

You're so cute, Tatsurou.

To Sagami, Tatsurou was like a wild dog who just needed some good training. Then he would be all Sagami's.

Sagami told Tatsurou what time to come to his apartment, then spent the rest of the day in eager anticipation.

As soon as the work day was over, Sagami burst out of the office and waited in his room. He had never waited for someone like this. It felt like a dream.

He had first met Tatsurou in high school, at a regional Kendo competition. People had always told him about another freshman who was as good as he was. When he finally saw Tatsurou, it was like an arrow shot to his heart.

He had also heard that Tatsurou attended one of the worst schools in the prefecture. So he was surprised to see his rival's rather small, innocent-looking face. The boy's appearance actually seemed to be in stark contrast to the stories told about him. As soon as their eyes met, he had felt something snap inside him. He just couldn't look away. Never before had someone had such an impact on him.

He had been so stunned by these strange new feelings, he didn't even acknowledge Tatsurou. Tatsurou had quickly looked away, completely uninterested in him. In Tatsurou's eyes, Sagami was nothing. The only way for Sagami to get Tatsurou's attention was to beat him. That was their first meeting.

When we were sophomores, something even more memorable happened.

Sagami remembered it vividly.

Tatsurou had been totally shocked when he had lost to Sagami the previous year. The next time he saw him, he yelled "This year, scum!"

Sagami's body had been filled with the excitement of that challenge. He felt that defeating Tatsurou was their special courtship, and gave his all to win that tournament. Tatsurou was good, as usual, and there were plenty of tense moments. It wasn't easy, but in the end, Sagami won.

Later, in the locker room, Sagami had glanced in Tatsurou's direction, but had no idea how to start a conversation. His mouth had dried up and he'd felt far too tense to make the words come out.

"Umm…" he'd mumbled nervously.

Tatsurou instantly turned around, looking humiliated and biting his lip. Sagami saw tears in Tatsurou's eyes.

Then Tatsurou took off without a word. But the boy had left a huge impression on Sagami, one he would never, ever forget.

At that precise moment, Sagami fell in love.

Tatsurou didn't.

But no matter. Whenever Sagami thought about that look on Tatsurou's face, his heart always beat a little faster. He was still immersed in his fantasy when the doorbell rang.

Sagami opened the door to find Tatsurou standing there. He wore a pure white suit, a red silk shirt, and a silver tie. Typically Yakuza, but that was what made Tatsurou sexy. He must have picked up the fierce expression from living with criminals.

I'm going to enjoy this so much.

Sagami had never met anyone as stimulating as Tatsurou. The man simply fascinated him.

"I thought you said this was walking distance from the factory," Tatsurou snapped, breaking the silence between them.

"Yeah," Sagami agreed. "This is Takanawa. But I have another place near the factory."

"Ah," Tatsurou said, looking unimpressed. The apartment was clearly not cheap, but hardly enough to excite him.

"Well, come in," Sagami said.

He had Tatsurou sit next to the piano. The man seemed bored by the piano, too. He just scowled at everything.

This isn't going to work.

Sagami pushed a contract he'd prepared toward Tatsurou.

"How much do you need?" he asked, staring at Tatsurou's profile. He softly ran his fingers down his own face, feeling the bandage at the side of his mouth. The cut from where Tatsurou had kicked him last night throbbed.

"Three million, no, eight million," Tatsurou stated, licking his lips.

"Eight million," Sagami echoed.

Tatsurou suddenly looked worried. Did Sagami even have that much?

Sagami took back the contract and jotted that number down.

"The security is, as we discussed, your body," he said.

It was very business-like. Tatsurou twitched like something inside him had been plucked. But Sagami knew Tatsurou had no choice. He saw Tatsurou's hand was tightly clenched from all the stress. So cute.

"Ah-huh," Tatsurou muttered.

"Your word is good, right?" Sagami said.

"Of course," Tatsurou said stiffly. He looked tense and very flustered.

Just seeing Tatsurou like this made it all worthwhile for Sagami. The money that would finance this loan was money he saved while training abroad.

He held out the contract. "Sign here. And then your name-stamp here. If not, a thumb print will do."

Sagami didn't expect to get the money back. If the man he loved needed it, he would lend it. But he guessed that Tatsurou had more of a conscience than he let on. If so, the documentation could come in handy for future "deals."

He must feel like a woman who's been forced into prostitution.

Sagami kept looking at Tatsurou, though he really tried not to. Tatsurou actually did bring his name-stamp. He really was a man of his word.

When the business was finished, Sagami carried the document to his safe. To him, it looked almost like a marriage license. He felt like he was floating on air.

Tatsurou gave him a sharp look. "What about the money?"

"I don't keep that much money here, of course," Sagami replied. "Tomorrow, when the banks open, we'll go get it. Don't worry. Tonight, you satisfy me."

Tatsurou frowned. What was he supposed to do now?

"Are you nervous?" Sagami asked, kneeling in front of Tatsurou. He moved his face closer to him.

Tatsurou looked away. Suddenly he felt Sagami's hot breath on his neck. He shivered and looked back at Sagami.

"Whoa," he stuttered, falling backward. After his head bounced off the floor, he tried to crawl away.

But Sagami had anticipated that move, and was already behind Tatsurou. He picked him up from behind and blew softly into his ear. Tatsurou's body tensed from head to toe.

"I never knew forcing a Yakuza to sleep with me could be this stimulating," Sagami whispered. "I'm definitely going to enjoy you."

"No, ah, I," Tatsurou stuttered.

Afraid that Sagami's breath might turn him on, Tatsurou quickly shook him off. Sagami seized the opportunity to fondle Tatsurou's ass.

"Ah!" Tatsurou yelled, trying to push Sagami away. But Sagami had no intention of releasing him. They fell back to the floor in a sweaty heap.

Sagami bent over Tatsurou and pinned him down. His muscles tensed, revealing their strength. Now that things were getting serious, Tatsurou started to scream with pain.

"It hurts! Let me go!"

Sagami lifted himself up. Tatsurou rubbed the inside of his elbow and looked up at Sagami from the floor.

This angle was perfect. Now that Tatsurou couldn't resist, maybe Sagami could bring the tears to his eyes that he so desperately needed to see.

"What the hell are you?" Tatsurou gasped.

"What do you mean?" Sagami asked.

"You didn't just do Kendo. You did something else, too," Tatsurou accused.

He really must have hurt Tatsurou.

Of course.

It was all for this day. He had trained for this day. He needed the knowledge so that he could overpower Tatsurou. Nothing could stop him now.

However, I don't want it to escalate.

He must never forget this was Tatsurou. If he did try to resist, he could get injured. Sagami definitely wanted him to cry, but not feel any actual pain.

He pushed down Tatsurou's wrists and lowered his face.

"Well, you guessed it," he said. "Kendo 4th degree belt. Judo 3rd degree belt. A little karate."

"Why?" Tatsurou asked with a frown.

Sagami shrugged. He could tell the truth, even though Tatsurou wouldn't accept it. "I enjoy it.

Reminds me of high school. I've been waiting for a good opponent."

He needed to use a little aggression first, before he could claim Tatsurou's body and heart.

"Let's do this," he suddenly said. He grabbed Tatsurou's wrist and led him to the bedroom. The sash from his bathrobe was on the bed.

"I'll tie your hands with this so you don't get hurt," he said seriously.

"Are you kidding me?" Tatsurou screamed.

"Promise not to resist me then?" Sagami said.

"No, look, calm down." Tatsurou winced. Sagami was scaring him a little.

"I'm calm. You're the one who's not," Sagami pointed out.

"No. Look, why do I have to sleep with you?" Tatsurou snapped.

Something had changed, but Tatsurou's angry voice was still adorable. Threats would not work. They would only get Sagami even more excited.

Sagami whispered gently in his ear, "You've already signed your body away."

Taking advantage of Tatsurou's shock, Sagami rolled him onto the bed. Tatsurou couldn't believe he was being treated like a young girl. He tried to sit up, but Sagami quickly leaned over him.

"Wait! Wait! Let's talk about this!" he pleaded.

"You don't know when to give up, do you?" Sagami taunted. He started to undo the buttons on Tatsurou's shirt. He'd never felt so excited undressing another person.

"You piece of shit," Tatsurou swore, trying to claw back some of his self respect.

Sagami said nothing.

"Whatever," Tatsurou spat out. "I'm a man. If you're gonna do me, do me! If you wanna tie me up, tie me up!"

"Well, then! I won't hold back," Sagami said.

Now everything was finally perfect, just what he wanted.

He tied Tatsurou's hands together like a sacrificial virgin—then bent down to taste his prize.

"Make as much noise as you want," Sagami said.

Tatsurou ignored him.

The front of his suit was open. All the buttons on his shirt had been undone. His pants were pulled down to his knees. He was powerless.

Sagami kissed him, then started stroking his body.

Tatsurou tried to resign himself to this, but still flinched every time Sagami touched him.

He was using every ounce of his energy to suppress his squeals and moans, while Sagami remained ever so calm. Tatsurou trembled all over, but could only endure the violations the other man forced upon him. He was terrified that his body would react positively to Sagami's advances.

"Tatsurou," Sagami whispered, pinching his nipples. "You sure are sensitive. They stand up like a girl's when I pull on them. It must feel good."

"I'll kill you, you bastard!" Tatsurou growled. But he'd been saying this all night.

The stimulation on his nipples sent little shocks through his body. His mind was swimming at Sagami's touch. He had never realized how much physical strength was required to keep sexual pleasure bottled up inside.

"Come on," Sagami coaxed. "Don't hold back on me. You know, I often thought about you when I jerked off back in high school. Did you do that? Tell me."

"As if I would! Ugh," Tatsurou retorted.

Sagami pulled on his nipple again. Tatsurou coughed to suppress his groan. He never knew his nipples could be this sensitive, but each time Sagami touched them, he felt more and more excited.

"Ngh…"

He tried to move away, but the rope on his wrists kept him in place. He told himself that being tied up naked was turning him on, not being with another man.

"Don't pretend you hate this," Sagami whispered. "This is quite a sensitive spot you have here. I'll be sure to look after it. You look like you could come now, just with your nipples."

Tatsurou felt humiliated. Just then, Sagami stroked his stomach, working down to his thigh. Sagami pulled Tatsurou's pants and underwear all the way down, and then slid his finger down the inside of Tatsurou's thigh.

"Ngh, ah," Tatsurou groaned, terrified that Sagami would touch his penis. Being touched by a guy was more than he could take. He snapped his legs shut, trying to shield his private parts from Sagami's probing hands.

Then the unbelievable happened. Sagami closed his mouth around Tatsurou's nipple. It was strange to be suckled like this, but it actually felt kind of nice. Sagami released the suction, filling Tatsurou's whole body with a wonderful sensation. Tatsurou felt shockwaves running through his body from his two nipples, one being sucked, the other pinched.

"Stop…stop…ngh…no…please…"

Tatsurou didn't realize he had started to moan. He had lost himself in the gentleness of Sagami's touch. The harder Sagami sucked, the more Tatsurou's penis started to stiffen.

"Ahhh." Tatsurou clenched his fists, digging his fingernails into his palms.

"Your body tells the truth, at least," Sagami said mildly.

Tatsurou just gasped.

"You're trembling all over," Sagami pointed out. "What's making you so excited? You're even leaking a little. It's okay if you want to come. Just make sure you scream out for me."

"You basta—"

Stopping himself from climaxing was Tatsurou's attempt to hold on to his last shred of pride and dignity. But Sagami kept on licking Tatsurou's nipples with a wide grin on his face. Tatsurou started panting again. He looked up at the ceiling.

"You're so stubborn," Sagami cooed, biting down on a nipple.

Tatsurou arched his back in reaction. "Ah!"

It was a mix of pain and pleasure. Sagami bit down again.

Tatsurou squealed in pain, mixed with even more pleasure. "N-no, don't bite," he begged, still trembling. He could take the pain, but the pleasure was almost too much for him.

"Tatsurou, you look so inviting," Sagami said. "You're really leaking now. Wanna see if you can come without my even touching it?"

His cruel words sounded far away now. Tatsurou knew he had to gain control somewhere, and clenched his teeth.

How?

Little tears streamed down his cheeks. Sagami couldn't see him like this. He tried to turn away, but Sagami was too strong. Again Sagami's lips made their way toward Tatsurou's nipples.

"AH!"

Once again, that sweet pain. Excitement and desire spread like an electric shock through Tatsurou's body. His entire body tensed—and then collapsed.

Tatsurou felt groggy. It was a totally different feeling from the raging peak of his climax. A warm afterglow of happiness spread throughout his body.

Now that his legs were raised in the air, he couldn't react at all. His knees were pushed up to his chest and his legs spread open. He had never been in this position before.

"What…" he mumbled.

He had had an idea of what sex between men was all about, but never imagined doing it himself. Just thinking about it made him tense up.

"You know what," Sagami said.

He scooped up some lubricant with his fingers and pushed it inside Tatsurou's hole.

"OW!" Tatsurou yelled.

This was the first time anyone's fingers had been inside him. He groaned as if Sagami was touching his deepest organs.

"Relax. This is so it won't hurt. Don't get tense. Just take a deep breath," Sagami instructed.

"What…" Tatsurou groaned.

Easy for him to say. It wasn't him about to get—

Tatsurou struggled to escape Sagami's probing fingers, but he could barely move. Sagami's martial arts skills completely overwhelmed him. His muscles tightened around the index finger inside him. He groaned at the painful sensation.

"It hurts!" he protested.

Each time Sagami moved his finger, Tatsurou's eyes filled with tears. He desperately tried to hide his face, even though his hands were still tied.

Five minutes later, Sagami pushed two fingers inside. The initial pain suddenly disappeared. To Tatsurou's surprise, his recently spent penis hardened again. Why did his body feel so excited? Tatsurou himself felt tired and pathetic. And there was nothing he could do but lie back and take it.

The fingers came out. Now that he was empty again, Tatsurou really felt his muscles twitching inside. Sagami noticed and laughed.

"Tatsurou," he purred, pushing three fingers in this time while he licked Tatsurou's ear. "You're opening up for me. Each time I move, you make those dirty noises."

Tatsurou wildly shook his head, but transparent liquid soon oozed from his penis.

What the hell is happening to me?

Sagami removed his fingers and made a little decisive nod. Tatsurou let out a little groan. Sagami's hard member rubbed against his thigh. Was this next?

"No, wait," he said desperately.

"For what?" Sagami asked, impatient.

"I…I can't do this," Tatsurou admitted, voice totally humiliated.

Sagami just laughed. He grabbed his own penis and stroked the tip, then opened Tatsurou's thighs, setting his sights on the main target.

"Look, I'll be gentle," he said. "Trust me, you'll really like it."

Tatsurou looked up, dying to say something vicious and cruel, like the gang member he was. But it was too late. He'd already sold his body to this man. Now he had to take it.

"Like I need gentle," he scoffed.

"Well, then! Shall I give you all I got?" Sagami said seductively. "I have some hard, *hard* evidence of my 10 years of love for you."

Love?

What was Sagami talking about? Tatsurou didn't have a clue. But when he looked at the weapon aimed in his direction, he hardened as well.

Bastard.

He swallowed hard. How could Sagami even think of pushing that up there? He had to be kidding! It would rip him apart. Tatsurou was scared shitless.

"Wait…wait a second…" he began to say.

Sagami completely ignored him. Grabbing Tatsurou's legs at the knees, he forcefully pushed his penis inside him. It stung like a steel pole. Though Sagami's fingers had loosened him up somewhat, nothing could have prepared Tatsurou for this.

"OW! You *BASTARD!* Get it out! Take it out!" he screamed, trying to move away. A sharp pain shot through him, like he was being ripped up inside. He gasped for breath.

"It only hurts the first time. You're all right." Sagami's low voice shook the very center of Tatsurou's being.

"I…can't…take…it…out…" he begged.

Sagami firmly pressed his lips against Tatsurou's, leaving no room for Tatsurou to even bite him. Suddenly Sagami darted his tongue into Tatsurou's mouth, licking and slurping. To cope with the pain down below, Tatsurou sucked on Sagami's lips.

"Ngh…"

Saliva flowed out of their mouths and rolled down their faces. Tatsurou's brain suddenly went numb. When he came to, Sagami's entire member was inside his body.

Finally they released lips. Tatsurou felt nothing in his crotch. He couldn't feel his own cock. Sagami slowly moved inside him, gripping Tatsurou's hips. It felt strange, like his insides were being dragged out with each stroke.

"Ah, ngh, ah…"

Sagami was grinding against Tatsurou with all his weight. Tatsurou felt each thrust opening him up more and more. That hurt the most now.

"Ow! Ngh…ah…ow."

Strange thing was, he was actually getting used to it. Sagami seemed to be holding back a bit, so it didn't hurt too much. Still, feeling this helpless was utterly humiliating. His body, conquered by another man. Even so, he was melting with pleasure.

SHIT! he screamed to himself.

He wanted to run away, but this feeling was swiftly taking him to new heights of perversion, like he was drugged or something.

Each time the penis pushed deep, Tatsurou gasped. With just a little force, Sagami could push himself all the way in. It unnerved Tatsurou, but Sagami didn't stop pounding. Instead, he just smiled.

"So tight," Sagami grunted.

"Shut…up…" Tatsurou groaned back.

He had felt a lot of foreign objects inside him today. And he had had enough, or so he thought.

"Just…get it over…with," he gasped, his voice betraying his excitement.

Sagami squinted at him. "Well then, just let me have a turn, okay?"

Now the in and out movements of Sagami's penis became much more forceful. Sagami pulled back his groin and then shafted Tatsurou all the way.

Tatsurou felt like he was going to be ripped up inside, but the feeling actually excited him. He felt almost numb.

"Ngh…ah…ah…do it!" he yelled.

"No more complaints?" Sagami managed to ask.

"It…hurts…" Tatsurou groaned.

"Come quick, Sagami. Stop hurting me, Sagami. All you do is complain," Sagami teased.

He was also panting hard, but paused for a moment to look down at Tatsurou.

His expression surprised Tatsurou. He simply oozed sexuality.

Am I falling for this guy?

Tatsurou blushed at the thought.

"How about *this* then?" Sagami grunted, pushing his penis hard inside Tatsurou. This time it hit a spot that had not been touched before. The feeling of being totally filled up made Tatsurou shiver.

"Ah!"

Tatsurou sucked in his breath at this violent feeling that he had never experienced before. Honey oozed from the tip of his penis.

"Here?" Sagami looked delighted, like he'd just found a precious jewel. He clamped his fingers onto Tatsurou's nipples again, then went back to work, pushing forcefully inside him.

"AH…AH…"

It felt so good! Tatsurou just couldn't resist anymore. Each time Sagami pushed in, he felt an ecstasy throughout his entire body, just like being high.

"Ngh…"

Tatsurou felt full, like he could come at any moment. The sensation was so overwhelming that his penis felt ready to spurt. Only his mind wasn't ready.

What is this?

Sex with a man? This wasn't possible. Tatsurou grimaced at the fact that his penis was erect and he was panting with excitement. Sagami's nipple-play made him even more crazed.

"Ah!"

Sagami grabbed Tatsurou's legs and folded up his body. He could get in deeper this way. The speed of the pounding increased.

"Ngh! No…ah! AH, ah!"

Tatsurou's insides made a sucking sound as Sagami's solid member pushed in and out. Tatsurou's mind went blank. He couldn't resist any more. He felt like he was about to overflow.

Just then, he sensed that Sagami was about to finally pull out. But the next thrust pushed deep inside.

"Ngh. Ah."

Sagami stopped.

Did he finally come? Tatsurou could feel Sagami's penis fluttering inside him. One second later, he felt his own orgasm. His mind drifted to a far away place.

Sagami relaxed, slumping his sweat-soaked body on top of Tatsurou's.

"Did you feel that…?" Sagami whispered.

His breath near Tatsurou's ear sent shockwaves through Tatsurou's body. He untied the rope that held Tatsurou's hands together.

He continued to whisper, "Pleasure makes you lose yourself. Beautiful oblivion."

But Tatsurou couldn't agree. It was true, what he had just felt was different from anything he had felt before. Just when he was coming, in that moment, all the blood in his body boiled over, and then there was that feeling as he scaled the summit…

"No. I didn't feel it," he said bluntly. But his legs were shaking.

Sagami was still buried deep inside him. Tatsurou wanted him to take it out, but didn't want him to know his body was still responding.

"Get the hell off! You weigh a ton," he snapped.

"No. This is amazing. Tatsurou, you were better than I had even imagined. I'll never forget it. You're a dream come true." Sagami brushed back his sweaty black hair and smiled his enigmatic smile. "Tatsurou, you're so sexy! I'm getting hard again."

"Fuck you! Get the fuck off!" Tatsurou screamed.

Sagami grabbed Tatsurou's arms. Tatsurou still had no feeling in his limbs and was powerless to stop him. So he relaxed, resigned to his fate.

And they did it again.

That was amazing.

Sagami stroked Tatsurou's hair as the man slept, and softly kissed him. Tatsurou wouldn't wake up for a while. Sagami had indulged himself until morning, and now Tatsurou was dead-tired.

Checking his watch, Sagami decided to phone Lovely's Kantou branch manager. He was an early bird and would probably be reading the newspapers right now. When Sagami was young, the man had often visited him. He was very loyal. Right now Sagami was below him in the hierarchy, but as soon as Sagami got used to the work, he would replace him as branch manager.

"Hey. It's me. Sorry to call you so early," he greeted the manager.

He watched Tatsurou's sleeping face as he talked on his cell. Sleeping with Tatsurou just once made Sagami want him even more. He wanted to bind Tatsurou to him tightly and never let him go.

"Yes, just like we discussed yesterday," he continued. "The Hinodegumi collection. No problem. I'll take full responsibility. Yes, the factory on the Arakawa. Whatever happens, it must be done cleanly."

Tatsurou wasn't really the Yakuza type. He was an honest, hard-working guy who had never really tossed his morals away. On the other hand, Sagami strove to make Lovely the best, even if it meant stooping to dirty deals. Sagami hoped to use Tatsurou's power to help Lovely grow.

When it came to the Uchida factory, Tatsurou would never collect that money. Those morals he still clung to got in the way.

He might ask Sagami for help again. And Sagami would help him. That was how he planned to keep Tatsurou coming back.

No matter what I have to do, I want to keep you by my side forever.

Just as Sagami hung up, Tatsurou started to move.

"Ngh…" Tatsurou mumbled, opening his eyes a crack. Sagami laughed out loud when he saw Tatsurou struggling to wake up.

"Wh-what, you jerk?" Tatsurou muttered.

"I just think you look cute," Sagami said. "Your money is ready for pick up when the bank opens. Just to let you know, there will be interest on that eight million. We need a million every month, plus interest. If you pay late, I intend to enjoy your body again."

"Huh?" Tatsurou winced.

He had hoped that last night would clear the debt once and for all. Sagami had originally thought so, too, but he hated to let go of such pleasure. Now that his appetite had been whetted, he'd put his bargaining tool to good use.

"You have to pay back what you borrowed," Sagami explained slowly. "Eight million is a lot of money."

He enjoyed teasing Tatsurou and pinched the other man's cheek.

"Fine," Tatsurou sighed.

Sagami could see that Tatsurou was livid, but he was not about to let this deal go. He was going to keep

Tatsurou, whether the man liked it or not.

I can't believe what happened yesterday.

Tatsurou sent Hachi off to the president with the money, then decided to take a nap.

He hurt. He didn't really want to stand. To be used like that, by someone not even in a gang! He was really starting to question his career choice. No doubt about it, Tatsurou was having a serious identity crisis this morning.

I need to toughen up.

He thought about his life as he lay limp on the sofa. Sagami had found ways to tease him because he was weak. He really had to work on his criminal image.

But people with money will always get their way.

Finding no answer to his woes, he fell asleep. Hachi came back into the office later and shook him awake. It was already dusk. The sky looked orange outside the window. Tatsurou took the phone from Hachi's hands.

"Good work, Tatsurou," the president said.

He had collected the ten million. The president was happy. Tatsurou heard something like a banquet going on in the background, most likely one of the Kantou Asahigumi's regular meetings. The Kantou Asahigumi operated above his gang, part of a long chain that passed demands down to each other.

"You know that factory you got the money from?" the president continued. "When I told Asahi you got ten million, they asked if you could get the money owed to them, too. Can you do something about it tonight?"

Not that place again.

Tatsurou gripped the phone. He had to think of something, but what?

"I, uh, don't think so," he bluffed. "He has no more mon—"

"Don't tell me it can't be done," the president interrupted coldly. "We can do things that can't be done, remember? That's why people come to us. Don't embarrass me, Tatsurou."

What the hell will I do?

Out of the frying pan and into the fire. This time he had no choice. He'd just have to get the money from Uchida.

I have to do it.

Tatsurou stood on the embankment and checked out Uchida's small factory. At first he hadn't seen what the fuss was all about. But now that the nearest train station had recently been improved, the demand for residential land around here would definitely increase. And people naturally wanted to build on the Uchida factory grounds.

I see.

Because of its value, the land had been used as collateral. Now, instead of collecting the loan, he needed to force Uchida to sign the land over. Someone else apparently had a claim to it, but that didn't matter to Tatsurou. This was a Yakuza's job. He just had to use his powers of persuasion.

I'll just have to do it.

It should have been an easy task for any hard-boiled gangster. But Tatsurou still had emotional ties to this place. If he had sorted this out from the start, he would have never been in this mess. He would have never needed Sagami's help.

But he couldn't be sentimental. He hadn't chosen the honest life. Tatsurou had to forget about Uchida.

Why me? I was just a stray dog!

Tatsurou had only been trouble for Uchida. Though Uchida had tried and tried to help him, Tatsurou had ignored it all.

"Showtime," he said to himself, stepping down from the embankment. There were lights on at Uchida's place, even at three in the morning. The other debt collectors had come and gone. Only Tatsurou had hung out this late.

Just then, a Lincoln Navigator came down the embankment road. Regular people didn't drive cars like that. It must be a gang leader. Tatsurou strained to see who was inside. The future successor to Lovely smiled at him through the window.

Tatsurou averted his eyes and quickened his pace, but the car stopped in front of him. Out stepped Sagami. Tatsurou glared at him, a blue vein visible on his forehead.

"What the fuck are you doing here?" he snapped.

Despite Tatsurou's look of pure loathing, Sagami kept on smiling.

"I know everything about you, Tatsurou," he said.

"I'll kill you," Tatsurou growled.

"Well I'll let you in on my trick this time," Sagami said. "I didn't want to drink alone, so I phoned your office. Some kid named Hachi picked up. When I asked him out for a drink, he told me about your ridiculous task here. Just thought I'd see if I could run into you."

"Goddamn Hachi," Tatsurou cursed. That idiot had loose lips. But then Tatsurou could probably never hide anything from a man like Sagami.

"I see. I don't have time to go drinking tonight. Get outta here," he snapped and started walking.

"I can't do that," Sagami retorted. "I have business here."

"What business?" Tatsurou asked.

"Collecting debt," Sagami replied. "Well, more like making sure it won't be dishonored."

"What debt?" Tatsurou asked.

"A body I need to protect," Sagami answered with a large grin. "You could call it my investment. If you needed another loan, Tatsurou, you could have come to me. The conditions might be a bit harsher than last time, but I would gladly help you out."

"What the fuck are you talking about?" Tatsurou screamed. "It's only a wrinkled old man."

Sagami just smiled. Tatsurou ignored him and walked on.

I'm a fucking hardcore criminal and he treats me like a girl.

Sagami was making a fool out of him again. Normally, people immediately kept their distance when they found out he was Yakuza. Any idiot knew not to mess with him.

Tatsurou circled the building. The lights were still on. He would show Uchida no mercy this time. No one would notice if anything unsightly happened here. The neighboring iron factory had been sold for development and was already being dismantled. The grass growing around it was up to his knees. The cop car from last time hadn't even shown up tonight. Tatsurou had no worries about attracting unwanted attention.

"Old man!" he yelled. "You there? Old man!"

He kicked on the door of a shabby house next to the factory, sensing Uchida was inside. He'd just kick until the old man came out. He had never come to Uchida's actual home before. Nothing much had changed from the days he had recovered here. But he firmly pushed down the memories that floated into his head.

The door opened.

"You again," Uchida grumbled.

He'd already doused Tatsurou twice now. Uchida probably recognized Tatsurou's face. The Yakuza saw a dark, dirty kitchen behind the old man.

"Go home already!" Uchida yelled. "I ain't giving my factory to you!"

Such a stubborn old man. He must be over 60 by now. It looked like he had already let his employees go. All of the shoes in the hallway must belong to Uchida. Since his son was killed in an accident, Uchida had no one in his life.

The old man looked haggard, probably from

chasing off the hordes of debt collectors. Tatsurou folded his arms and softened a little.

"Just listen, old man," he said. "I'm here for a different debt. You owe ten million to Hanamura Finance. Look, here's the document. You must remember borrowing it. You have to pay back what you borrow. You honor your word, don't you?"

"I won't give up this place," Uchida said stubbornly. "I don't care how many times you come. I won't give my factory to anyone!"

"This rundown dump?" Tatsurou sneered. "What good is it? That big factory took all the work. You could retire, take life easy! I could help you get some money together."

He talked, pleaded, and cajoled for at least three minutes, but Uchida would have none of it.

"I was tricked. I didn't borrow that money," the old man kept repeating. "They made me sell off my equipment. They stopped the contract. Just kill me, all right?"

They really had gone after Uchida. But Tatsurou had heard many sob stories like this and no longer felt sad about them.

Sagami, who had been standing behind Tatsurou the whole time, suddenly spoke up. "But why can't you leave?" he said.

Uchida glared at Sagami and then looked back at Tatsurou. A light of compassion glittered in his eyes.

"I can't leave this place. I made a promise," he simply said.

"A promise?" Tatsurou echoed.

Uchida looked behind Tatsurou, a twinkle in his bloodshot eyes.

"Long ago, I worked as a probation officer, helping wayward kids," he explained further. "I told them if they ever had nowhere to go, they could always come here. They're all grown up now, maybe married, got kids, who knows. But in case they slip up, they still need a place to come to. They can't come back here and find nothing."

Tatsurou felt as if his heart had been ripped out. All the blood drained from his head. Was Uchida saying this because one of those kids was standing before him right now? But the old man didn't make a move.

"Oh?" said the voice behind him.

Tatsurou turned around and ran.

"I'll be back! Then I'll force you to sign!"

Those were his last words as he dashed away.

"I've been looking for you."

Tatsurou had fallen asleep on the bank, looking up at the sky. Sagami showed up a while later and sat down next to him. Tatsurou still felt awful.

"He didn't notice," he said suddenly.

"Huh?"

"The old man," Tatsurou clarified. "He didn't notice I was one of those kids. He said he was a probation officer."

A probation officer watched over wayward kids until they were rehabilitated. But the police had never caught Tatsurou back then, so he had never met

Uchida as a probation officer. Their meeting was entirely coincidental. Tatsurou had never even known Uchida did that kind of work.

"Of all the kids Uchida worked with, I was definitely the worst. Now I'm a worthless scum. If Uchida ever found out, he'd probably wish he'd never helped me. It wouldn't matter that I looked like his son. In fact, that would only make it worse."

A vacant smile spread over Tatsurou's face.

He had always wanted people to fear him. He thought his Yakuza life fulfilled that dream. So why did his heart feel torn to pieces by some old man? He knew talking to Sagami wouldn't help, but he couldn't stop baring his soul.

"I understand why the old man's so stubborn," he continued. "But it's pointless, isn't it? No one will come back to find him now. Who's he waiting for, anyway? No one. No one." His voice faded into the darkness.

Finally Sagami spoke. "He wants to be useful to someone, anyone. He realizes there's no point now, but he still thinks he can help. And that alone keeps him going, keeps him happy."

Sagami didn't need to tell Tatsurou all this. Tatsurou already knew. Even though he had taken a completely different path in life, he still understood the old man.

Intimidation would not work with Uchida. In fact, nothing would. The days when Tatsurou only had to issue fierce threats were over.

He glanced over at Sagami, remembering how it felt when their skins touched. He had only slept with this man once, but he was already addicted. Make no mistake, he still hated Sagami. But he was feeling so depressed and so lonely right now, he wanted Sagami by him.

Sagami continued in his soft voice, "But Mr. Uchida must have remembered you! Those eyes make you look like a stray wildcat. People never forget guys like you. Plus you lied to him way back then. He would definitely remember that."

"Don't wanna hear it," Tatsurou muttered.

Now Sagami copied Tatsurou and sprawled on the bank. He crossed his arms under his head and looked up into the night.

"Nope, he didn't remember me," Tatsurou went on. "But he doesn't have to wait for me or anyone else. He should move to the country and plough fields or something."

"Why not tell Mr. Uchida that you have no regrets?" Sagami suggested. "Say you were one kid he helped out. Tell him that you've chosen a gangster's life and you don't need his help. Then he can stop waiting. Maybe he'll give up and leave."

"Ugh," Tatsurou snorted, lighting a cigarette. In the darkness, the flame glowed orange. He zoned out, watching the smoke rise into the air.

Sounded like a good plan. But even though Tatsurou would have loved to make that speech, he just couldn't. He stared up at the starless, cloudy sky. Sagami had nothing else to say.

As dawn drew near, Tatsurou, shivering, decided it was time to go home. He glanced over at Sagami, who was sleeping peacefully.

Should I just leave him here?

He took a blanket from his car, covered Sagami with it, and left. He felt like he had done a good deed, plus he didn't want to hear Sagami griping that he caught a cold.

In the days that followed, Tatsurou often visited Uchida. And Sagami would also visit Tatsurou, now that he had a debt with Lovely.

Tatsurou tried to chase him away, but since his gang was affiliated with Lovely, he couldn't use violence. It was really annoying. Sagami chatted with Hachi and asked Tatsurou how everything was.

It was near the end of November now.

Tatsurou kept threatening, but Uchida still wouldn't leave. He kept wanting to reveal himself to the old man, but never seemed to find the guts to do so.

"Tatsurou. You're taking your time over this one," the president reminded him one day.

Tatsurou's body tensed. "I'm sorry. He's a stubborn bastard."

"Are you doing what you have to do?" the president wanted to know. "Do you really know how to push him? Brute strength always works best. Throw a dead dog through the window at dinnertime. That will get rid of him."

"Sir, he really is a stubborn bastard!" Tatsurou insisted.

"If that doesn't work, mix paint with shit," the

president said. "Spread it everywhere. He won't get over that easily."

Times really had changed. They never used to stoop to such tactics. Now the gang would do anything it took to get the money.

"I just need a little more time," Tatsurou bargained.

"Ah. But don't keep me waiting too long. I can't lose face here." The president coughed before he continued in a darker voice. "If you have no other choice, burn the joint."

"Burn it?" Tatsurou gasped.

"Yes, a grand gesture to get the money repaid," the president answered. "But if you can't do it, you know what I'll have to do to you."

With that threat, the president hung up.

While Tatsurou was lost in his thoughts, Sagami sat next to him.

"Not a good conversation, eh?" Sagami remarked. "If you're still having money problems, my company can offer you another loan."

"Really?" Tatsurou asked, blushing.

It would definitely be better than burning the place down. His heart beat a little faster.

"But the conditions will be harsher than last time," Sagami said mysteriously.

"How so?" Tatsurou asked warily.

Sagami grinned. "First, move in with me. It'll be eight million. You can't run away."

"I won't run away," Tatsurou snapped.

"But if we live together," Sagami went on,

"I'll have to take out your share of the expenses. Rent, electric bills…"

"What the fuck are you talking about?!" Tatsurou screeched.

Sagami was sounding like they'd be newlyweds!

"We'll add it to the other conditions," Sagami said calmly, pulling a contract from his pocket. "Just sign next to the living together part."

"Like hell I'll live with you! But I'll take a look at it," Tatsurou grumbled, eyeing Sagami suspiciously. He took one look at the contract and ripped it apart.

"Ah!" Sagami cried out in dismay.

"You bastard!" Tatsurou yelled. "What the hell is this? Three fingers up the ass?!"

He tossed the shredded contract into the ashtray and lit it with his lighter. He couldn't rely on Sagami. He had to do something himself.

I have to burn the place down.

He couldn't go against the president. Underlings did what they were told. All this worrying about it wasn't doing any good.

I have to do it!

Tatsurou was a gangster. He couldn't go back. He could only go forward.

The memory of Uchida's face still made him feel sick. But today he would say goodbye to his old, emotional self.

"Well?" Tatsurou crossed his arms and glared

at Sagami, who was sitting beside him. "Why the hell are you still here? You had some food. Shouldn't you go home?"

It was two in the morning.

Behind Tatsurou's Benz, which was parked on the bank, was Sagami's Lincoln Navigator.

Tatsurou looked hesitant. It was only natural. Sagami had turned up just as he was about to commit arson.

Sagami smoothly got out of his car and gave him a bewitching smile.

"Today is debt collection day, remember?" he said. "I've been stuck in the office, so I thought I'd get some fresh air."

He knew all about Tatsurou's plan. Not only did Hachi have a big mouth, he was also an excellent source of information on the Hinodegumi and its parent group, the Asahigumi.

Just because he knows, doesn't mean he can stop me.

Tatsurou was so stubborn. Sagami worried that if he didn't keep an eye on him, he would lose his investment. And today he planned to really cement their relationship.

"I'm here to collect the debt you owe me," he said.

Tatsurou looked startled. He'd been so busy planning the arson, he had totally forgotten.

Sagami wanted Tatsurou to pay back his debt with his body, but he just hinted at it.

"It's been a long day," Sagami continued. "Once

a month, a million yen. I should have collected once or twice a week. Shame."

"Go home! I have no money to give you!" Tatsurou yelled, suddenly defiant. Sagami wanted to play it nice tonight, but Tatsurou clearly didn't want to be touched. He was getting tougher. A man's pride was precious and not easily broken down.

"Go home, Tatsurou," Sagami said not unkindly. "You're playing kid's games here."

"Shut the hell up! You always get in my way when it comes to making money!" Tatsurou retorted.

"Always?" Sagami echoed. He frankly didn't remember another time.

Tatsurou was getting sick of the continuous questions. "In high school! Our second year! If I had won that competition, I would have gotten the prize money! But you robbed it from me! Ten thousand is a lot for a kid!"

Sagami was stunned. Seeing Tatsurou cry after he lost was the moment Sagami fell in love with him. He reached for Tatsurou's chest and forcefully pushed it against the car.

Tatsurou felt a burning passion inside. He was always suffering, but never wanted to break the bonds of his own torment. He lived only for the moment. He frowned. Sagami was pushing down too hard on him. His expression took Sagami's breath away.

"I've been really looking forward to today's collection, and I won't take no for an answer," Sagami breathed. "We both know I'm stronger than you. I'll drag you home if I have to."

"Fucking bastard!" Tatsurou's eyes were on fire.

He pushed himself off the car and lunged at Sagami. Sagami jumped back, dodging a fierce kick. Just then, Hachi showed up, breaking the tension.

"Sir! What time are we doing this?" the henchman asked eagerly.

Tatsurou kicked the dirt in frustration.

Uchida's neighbors had noticed his debt collector troubles and had invited him on a community trip. Sagami knew this, too. Uchida didn't go out much. Tatsurou felt this was his only chance.

"Hachi, leave the stuff there, and take Sagami away," he ordered.

"Huh?" Hachi asked.

"Get out of here. Sagami will pay for dinner and drinks. Eat all you want, he's loaded!" Tatsurou spat out.

"Really? But he's always bringing us food as it is," Hachi protested, looking up at Sagami. He was no junkyard dog like Tatsurou. He was an obedient puppy.

Tatsurou wanted to get rid of Sagami, who suspected Tatsurou didn't want Hachi involved in his crime.

But Sagami had been prepared for this, and would exit quietly for once.

"Fine. But only if Tatsurou promises to come over later," he said.

Tatsurou turned away from them. "When I have the money ready, then I'll meet up with you."

"You'll really come?" Sagami pushed.

Tatsurou smiled broadly. "Not me. You can have my cute employee instead."

At that moment, Sagami was dying to hold him. Teach him how to trust and be trusted.

I guess you feel you have no choice. That's how you've always lived.

Their lives were just too different. Sagami would never understand Tatsurou's hard life. But he still wanted to hold Tatsurou, be gentle with him. He wanted to be Tatsurou's safety zone.

But he's not ready yet.

He wasn't used to human company yet. He needed to be tamed like a wild beast.

Tatsurou glared at Sagami. He had already made up his mind. Arson was a crime. If they investigated, his name would come up. Even if there was no evidence, the police would never let it go. They would pull him in for something in the end.

I won't let that happen.

Sagami wanted to stop him, but he knew Tatsurou would just act even more defiant. No way would he listen to Sagami now.

Will they take you away from me? Sagami thought as their eyes met. He would make Tatsurou his pet without putting a chain on him. He would train him, win him over.

Tatsurou raised an eyebrow and averted his eyes, disturbed at the troubled look on Sagami's face. Sagami grimaced and chased away the images in his head. Tatsurou wasn't used to being tamed like this.

"Well, see you, boss!" Hachi shouted cheerfully,

climbing into the passenger seat. The Lincoln Navigator pulled away.

See you soon, Sagami thought wistfully. He had no intention of leaving Tatsurou alone tonight.

Tatsurou squeezed the gasoline bottle, watching the car retreat into the night. Then he turned to face the factory.

He took out a cigarette, lit a match—then suddenly remembered he was carrying gasoline. He'd have a smoke on the bank first. After all, he only intended to start a small fire, one which wouldn't spread.

That would be plenty enough. He only wanted to scare the old man. He could do this alone, without getting Hachi involved. If all went well, he wouldn't get caught.

Sorry, old man. Sorry I became a thug.

Since meeting Uchida and Sagami, Tatsurou's normal state of mind had completely crumbled. Why did it feel so strange to have other people care about him?

He wasted an hour lying on the bank, trying to steel himself for the task. He counted the few visible stars, then finally headed for the factory.

The building was shrouded in silence, except for the noise from an occasional passing taxi. Tatsurou looked around for cop cars, then dived under the open shutter doors to the factory.

Huh?

He sensed something was wrong and switched on the flashlight.

"Aaah!" he screamed, dropping the bottle of gasoline.

Someone was standing right in front of him.

"Sir! It's me!" Hachi yelled, picking up the bottle.

"Idiot! You scared me!" Tatsurou growled, his heart beating wildly.

Why the hell was Hachi here? Tatsurou had a bad feeling about this. If Hachi was here, then it was very likely someone else was, too.

"I suppose Sagami is here as well?" Tatsurou snapped, his voice echoing in the empty factory.

He swung the flashlight around. Suddenly he felt a warm breath on the back of his neck and jumped with surprise.

"You found me," Sagami said cheerfully.

"You jerk! Don't get in my fucking way!" Tatsurou screamed.

"You're late," Sagami said. "Hachi and I have been drinking here. But I'm not leaving until you pay your debt. One day late and you'll pay with your body…"

"What the fuck? Just shut the hell up!" Tatsurou hissed, not wanting Hachi to hear. He glanced down at the mess they'd made. Must have been a real party. Unbelievable.

Just then, Tatsurou realized he didn't just smell alcohol. The air was rank with the odor of gasoline. Suddenly he felt scared.

"Hachi! What the hell are you doing?" he yelled.

The acrid smell made him feel dizzy. Shining the

flashlight on the ground, he saw dark liquid spreading across the floor.

"You said you wanted to start a fire, sir," Hachi said drunkenly, staggering as he swung the bottle.

"You fucking idiot! What the hell do you think you're doing?! If you light it now, we'll all die!" Tatsurou continued to yell frantically.

"But, sir! You wanted a big, wonderful fire…" Hachi insisted.

"I was exaggerating!" Tatsurou said.

But Hachi was really out of it. Tatsurou saw a glowing cigarette dangling between his lips. The bastard would get them all killed! But before Tatsurou could scream a warning, the cigarette fell from Hachi's mouth.

In the next instant, the entire floor was covered in blue flames.

"I'm so sorry, sir! Siiir! Siiiir!" Hachi kept screaming, out of his mind with guilt.

Tatsurou grabbed him and fled the factory with Sagami. They all seemed fine, but maybe they just couldn't feel the pain yet.

When they reached a safe distance, Tatsurou turned back to look at the factory. Huge plumes of smoke billowed from the windows, while sparks scattered across the ground. It was only a matter of time before the whole building turned into a giant bonfire.

Sagami phoned the fire department and then hung up the phone.

"Hope the old man wasn't in there," he said grimly.

Nearby, some old women had gathered. They were talking about the old man. Hachi asked them about Uchida. They told him he was supposed to be away on a trip.

So the old man was gone...

"But I heard he suddenly got sick and couldn't go," a woman said sadly. "Hope he got out. Hope he got out okay."

"Oh, my. I do hope he's okay," another woman fretted.

Tatsurou heard them muttering to each other.

Was he sleeping inside?

Now Hachi was sprawled on the ground in a daze. Tatsurou grabbed his neck and shook him viciously.

"Bastard! You said the old man wasn't inside!" he screamed.

"Huh? He's not, I'm sure," Hachi answered, bewildered.

"He is in there. They said he was sleeping," Tatsurou growled.

Before he realized what he was doing, Tatsurou moved into action. He spotted some buckets, filled them with water, and poured it over his head. This was the third time he'd been soaked from head to toe in this place.

His body shook with the cold as he ran toward the factory. He would not let Uchida die in there.

"Tatsurou! Tatsurou, wait!" Sagami cried out from behind him.

Tatsurou didn't have time to listen right now. He dashed around the factory to get to Uchida's home. His dripping wet suit slowed him down, but he finally made it. He was relieved to see the fire hadn't reached the house yet. He kicked the door down and ran inside. Thick black smoke obscured everything.

"Old man!" he yelled. "Old man! Are you in here?!"

He ran to the kitchen, then the bathroom. He looked for Uchida in every room on the first floor, then tore up the narrow stairs, two at a time.

"Old man!" he called out. "Are you up here?"

His vision got more and more clouded by the black smoke, but the rooms looked empty. He pulled off the blankets on the bed. Uchida wasn't there, either.

Is he in the factory?

Tatsurou tumbled down the stairs and dashed outside. He took a deep breath and surveyed the scene before him. It was an inferno, but it wouldn't stop him from saving Uchida. He kicked open the factory door.

"Ah!" he cried out.

He immediately sensed something unusual was happening.

An explosion?!

The flames came at him like they were alive. Then he heard a loud, earth-shaking roar and knew for sure that something had exploded in the factory.

No way could he rescue Uchida now. The worst had happened.

He panicked and tried to flee. But he couldn't see through the smoke and it was getting harder and harder to breathe.

What the hell do I do now?

He covered his mouth with his sleeve, making breathing a little easier. His suit was still wet, so he didn't feel the heat, but his head was pounding like he was drunk.

He got on his knees and crawled to avoid breathing in more smoke. He had lost all sense of direction. He knew he didn't have much time left. It was difficult getting oxygen into his lungs. At last, he couldn't move anymore, and simply cowered next to a wall.

"Dammit…" he whimpered.

Unable to call for help, he felt himself losing consciousness.

"So this how I'm gonna die…"

To die so young. He silently wished his life could have been better.

Like you…

Suddenly an image of Sagami floated in his mind's eye. So what people always said was actually true—when your life is in grave danger, you'll be seized by sexual urges. He felt passion rising in his body.

He had never known how nice it was to be touched by another man. The feeling was strangely overwhelming. If he died now, he would never reach that climax again.

"Sagami, you bastard," he muttered. "Why the hell are you here in my dying moments…"

He remembered how it had felt when Sagami touched him. Would that be his last thought as he departed this world?

His eyes still closed and body motionless, Tatsurou heard Sagami's voice saying, "What are you doing?"

But it was only an illusion. If he was hearing things now, then he must be close to death.

Just then, someone pulled on his limp arm. Tatsurou tried to open his eyes, but his head hurt too much.

"Are you…real…?" he gasped.

Suddenly, someone pulled him into their arms. Tatsurou buried his face into Sagami's chest.

"What do you think?" Sagami rumbled.

"You can't be…real. I'm…dreaming," Tatsurou muttered. "The real Sagami is safe. He's watching the fire. He's probably worrying…about the eight… million…I owe…him."

"Sounds like the real me is pretty cruel," Sagami snorted, hoisting Tatsurou's body onto his back.

Each time Sagami took a step, Tatsurou felt comforted. Maybe dying wasn't so bad after all.

"Sagami," he said. "I don't have…life insurance."

"That's a shame," Sagami gasped. "What did you want to do?"

Tatsurou just smiled happily, resting on Sagami's back. Sagami was much stronger than he even remembered. Tatsurou felt secure with Sagami's hands around his thighs.

I want Sagami to do bad things to me. I must be a really bad person.

"Sex. I wish…I wish we'd…done it…once more…before I died," Tatsurou mumbled.

"Do you know that I love you?" Sagami asked.

"Not love…your body…is enough," Tatsurou said.

He didn't understand love. If he did, he would never have become a Yakuza.

Listening to Sagami's voice felt good. The sound melted into Tatsurou's eardrum. He wanted to hear this voice forever.

"When we get out of here, will you date me?" Sagami asked.

There was no doubt that this Sagami was just a figment of Tatsurou's imagination. The real Tatsurou was dreaming of being rescued by Sagami while being consumed by the flames. He smiled when he realized what was deep inside his heart.

"Taking advantage, aren't you? Of this emergency…" he mumbled.

"You'd never make me such a promise at any time other than this," Sagami pointed out. "So? Will you date me?"

He felt Sagami stop.

Fool.

Tatsurou pushed his cheek against Sagami's back.

His head felt foggy. If the Sagami-illusion didn't talk, he found it difficult to stay awake.

"If we…get out," he promised.

Just then he heard a rumbling sound. The sirens of the fire trucks were coming closer. But it was already too late.

Tatsurou opened his eyes a little and noticed Sagami had stopped moving. Suddenly, he saw Uchida's room. They were blocked by a wall of fire.

This is really happening!

The dreamlike feeling instantly disappeared. Sagami had run into the burning building to save Tatsurou!

"Sagami. You shouldn't have," Tatsurou scolded in a quiet voice.

Now Sagami would die, too. Tatsurou couldn't move, that was dead certain. But at least Sagami could run away to save himself.

"Get out…go," Tatsurou ordered. "Leave…me. I'm a…goner…"

He could only think of Sagami's escape. Sagami wasn't injured yet and could still move on his own. Tatsurou was just heavy baggage.

Sagami shook his head. When he met Tatsurou's eyes, he smiled gently.

"I can't do that, you're uninsured," he said. "If you die here, it would be a massive loss to Lovely."

His voice still sounded calm and gentle and full of love.

Suddenly, something collapsed nearby, pushing Sagami to the ground. Tatsurou knew the flames were coming closer. Then something else collapsed. Sagami pushed Tatsurou to the floor. It was getting even harder to breathe now, and he felt his consciousness drifting further away.

Just then, he felt Sagami's body over him, shielding him from danger. To be held like this made Tatsurou feel content, even in the middle of a disaster. He felt absolutely smothered in love.

Sagami's lips touched his. With the kiss of life, he breathed air into Tatsurou's lungs.

"I'll share my oxygen with you," Sagami whispered.

But Tatsurou just wanted Sagami to run away as fast as possible. Why should Sagami even save him? He had never done a single thing in his life that was worthwhile.

Tatsurou felt the end was coming, but he wasn't that scared. He had been prepared for death ever since he had become a Yakuza.

He couldn't restart his life now. He couldn't press a reset button. This was the end.

With a little oxygen in his lungs again, Tatsurou suddenly recalled what he was doing here in the first place.

The old man, is he all right?

Nothing was real anymore. He never wanted to become this scum who threatened people and ripped them off. He had wanted to hide himself from Uchida, so the old man never found out the painful truth.

But why was Sagami still here in his thoughts? For some reason, Sagami had managed to gently crack open the walls around his heart.

"Wh-why…?" Tatsurou sobbed.

It had been years since he'd cried like this, back when he felt completely, utterly alone.

He felt Sagami's lips again, blowing air into his empty lungs. The oxygen also brought warmth. He felt full of life, like a newborn child.

If I survive…

If he did, maybe he could start again. Give up his Yakuza life. Maybe he could bravely step back into the real world and find the happiness he always longed for.

Just as he slipped out of consciousness, Tatsurou heard Sagami's voice.

"Tatsurou, don't cry," the man said. "Seeing you cry makes me never want to leave you. You know, I never wanted to leave you in the first place."

Tatsurou came to on a hospital bed.

Hachi jumped up in excitement. He looked like he'd been crying.

"This is great!" he said. "Sir! You're on the news! A live broadcast, a newsflash! You were in the newspapers, too! I cut them out for you. You even made it into the sports papers!"

As Hachi excitedly babbled on, Tatsurou gradually figured out what must have happened. What had started off as local news, soon made its way to the national networks. The media had jumped on the breathtaking tale of two brave men escaping a burning building.

"A guy from another gang recorded it on video," Hachi continued. "I'll show you! Here, watch!"

He replayed the story on a television next to the

bed. In the video, two men emerged from the burning building. Both had coats over their heads and were covered in soot, so Tatsurou couldn't determine who was who. But Sagami had definitely risked his life to save him.

A reporter's voice narrated, "One man who ran into the smoke-filled building was a gang member. Now he's out. Oh. It's two men. There are two men. Looks like they've escaped unharmed."

So a gang member had run into a burning building. What a story. It had catapulted him into the news, if only for a short time. Soon, some financial scandal involving a well-known politician took the spotlight. So his story was now old news, much to Hachi's annoyance.

Tatsurou, still dazed from just waking up, was finding it hard to take in all this new information. Just then, Hachi's cell phone rang.

"Boss, it's the president."

Tatsurou took the phone and heard a loud scream.

"You, Tatsurou! What the fuck were you thinking?"

"Huh?" was all Tatsurou could say.

"You asshole!" the president cursed. "The Kantou Hinodegumi is a *gang*. Gang members don't get rescued! You made us look like wimps—we're the fucking laughingstock of all Japan!"

The president was definitely angry. Tatsurou heard him throwing something across the room.

"You are no longer a member of the Kantou

Hinodegumi," the president barked. "This is it. You have no connection with us. And if you give our name to the media, this won't be the end of it."

The president raged on some more, then finally hung up.

Tatsurou was stunned.

"Is the president mad?" Hachi asked innocently, taking back his phone. "Lots of people have called about you."

The Yakuza hated being ridiculed. But even if Tatsurou said the whole thing was a big lie, he still couldn't go back to the gang.

What was happening to him? Had he been reborn in the fire? He was finally free, and he didn't even have to lose a finger.

Tatsurou started to laugh.

"Not bad," he said.

"Huh? What do you mean, sir?" Hachi asked.

"I'm not in the gang anymore, he fired me," Tatsurou announced. "If you wanna keep your job, you'd better get over to his office."

"No! My place is with you! If you go, so will I. I'll follow you anywhere!" Hachi declared passionately.

"Don't be such an idiot!" Tatsurou lifted himself up on the bed to get a better shot at Hachi's head.

Just then the door opened, and in walked Sagami. As soon as he saw him, Tatsurou's heart skipped a beat, but he avoided direct eye contact.

Sagami gently called out, "Uh, Hachi, can you give us a minute? I need to talk to Tatsurou."

"Sure. See you tomorrow, sir! We can talk about

it then!" Hachi said with a wave. He was still loyal, despite Tatsurou's brand-new lack of power.

"What does he want to talk about?" Sagami asked with interest.

He's wearing a suit. He must not be a patient here.

"Nothing, really," Tatsurou replied. "Is the old man all right?"

"Turns out Mr. Uchida was never there in the first place," Sagami said.

"Huh?" Tatsurou gasped, raising his eyebrows.

Sagami sat on a stool by the bed and crossed his long legs. "Lovely gets a lot of information, not just on your Hinodegumi, but on the Asahigumi, the group above you. One of their members leaked the order to burn Mr. Uchida's factory. I knew you wouldn't listen to me, so I decided to keep quiet and see what happened. The day you were planning to make your move, I found Mr. Uchida in bed with a cold. I took him away. Caused some trouble, didn't you, Tatsurou?"

"So you knew everything?" Tatsurou asked incredulously.

"I only checked to make sure everything would be safe," Sagami said. "But I didn't predict that Hachi would get drunk and spill the gas, or that you would run into the burning building. I called out for you to stop, but you didn't hear me. As soon as I realized that, I ran in after you."

"Oh, I see," Tatsurou mumbled. "I should say sorry."

"No need to be sorry," Sagami said. "I want something else."

He stood up and moved his face toward Tatsurou, then suddenly grabbed his wrists. Tatsurou tried to throw him off, but Sagami was already straddling him.

The Judo expert's pinning technique simply overpowered him. As Sagami held him down, Tatsurou felt something in his underwear move.

"Bastard! What are you doing?" he gasped.

"Remember why I came to meet you that day?" Sagami said. "I was there to collect payment. You agreed to pay with your body if you had no money. Actually, I think you quite liked the idea."

He pulled a rubber tourniquet from his pocket, then tied Tatsurou's hands to the metal bars of the bed.

"I only came here to visit, but after seeing you, I can't hold back," he continued. "You're so exciting. Just before you almost died, you said you wanted me, remember?"

Tatsurou had a very vague memory of saying something like that.

"As if! It was all a mistake!" he protested.

"For a mistake, you sounded very serious," Sagami retorted.

"And anyway, if you only came to visit, aren't you a little over-prepared?" Tatsurou pointed out.

"Ah, that." Sagami smirked. "While I waited for you to wake up, I remembered your sweet words of love. I couldn't stop fantasizing, so I stole this thing from the nurse's cart. You've turned me into a thief, Tatsurou. You're totally to blame."

He stroked Tatsurou's nipples over his hospital robe. Tatsurou instantly tensed up.

Under the soft cloth, he could feel the numbness spreading. His little nipples were hardening. Giving in to Sagami's touch, Tatsurou felt a moan about to escape.

"What…what are you doing…ngh," he groaned.

His mind went blank. His body had experienced this once before. For some reason, being dominated by someone was a turn-on for him. His breathing turned to excited gasps. He couldn't believe he was enjoying this.

I can't let this bastard do what he wants!

Sagami parted the hospital robe, revealing Tatsurou's chest, and nibbled on the little pink nipples. Tatsurou stifled another moan.

"Wait. I'm…injured…ah."

"You only inhaled smoke," Sagami said. "You didn't get burned, and I'm so glad. No marks on your beautiful skin."

"I said stop!" Tatsurou protested.

Now Sagami rubbed Tatsurou's penis with his other hand. Tatsurou writhed. His nipples were so weak. When they were fondled, he couldn't think of anything else.

"Mr. Uchida?" he gasped.

His nipples became numb as Sagami licked them. He wanted them sucked so hard they hurt.

Sagami went from nipple to nipple, teasing Tatsurou.

"He says hello to you, by the way," he said between licks. "He knew all along you were the kid who ran away. He was just being stubborn. Mr. Uchida watched the news about you with tears streaming down his eyes. He knew you couldn't be all bad."

As Sagami spoke, the tip of his tongue flicked Tatsurou's nipples. Tatsurou's spine tingled with each flick. His body shook. It took supreme effort to listen to what Sagami was saying.

"What does that mean?" he gasped. "What... ah..."

"Lovely bought the factory from Mr. Uchida, so you don't have to worry," Sagami explained. "All his money problems have been sorted out. He also left me his new address, so you can visit him sometime soon."

"Ah," Tatsurou sighed.

When he was well again, he would go and say hello. He might not be able to work at the old factory, but he still wanted to tell Uchida he was working hard.

A pleasant feeling radiated in his crotch. Tatsurou arched his back, signaling Sagami to suck harder. Sagami gladly obliged.

"AH!"

Sagami sucked hard, like a baby feeding on a breast. There was pain, but even more pleasure. A hot sensation ran through Tatsurou's blood, melting his muscles.

"Ah...ngh.... Oh, uh..."

He couldn't stop himself. Each time Sagami sucked, he felt a sense of unity, like he was a partner in crime. Tatsurou's heart filled with love.

"Why are you...why do you help me?" he gasped out.

"Still don't get it, huh?" Sagami asked gently.

"How should I..." Tatsurou began.

"That's fine," Sagami said. "Don't even try to

understand. That's the Tatsurou I've grown to love."

Sagami quickly stripped him, then pulled Tatsurou's legs wide open with his strong arms. Tatsurou felt embarrassed to be splayed out like that before Sagami.

"You bastard!" he cried out.

He wanted to lash out, but couldn't.

"You look good," Sagami said.

Tatsurou already felt penetrated, just by Sagami's gaze. His legs quivered and he felt hot, despite the cold air. Just by being admired, his shame turned to joy. His penis became erect, its tip throbbing.

Just then, there was a strange sound. Tatsurou's whole body shook. He concentrated on what Sagami was touching and in the next movement, he knew.

"Uh," he managed to say.

Sagami had buried his finger into Tatsurou's body. Tatsurou's muscles sharply contracted, pulling down on Sagami's finger. The finger was thrust deep inside him and moving around.

Tatsurou groaned at being touched like that. Sagami slowly twisted his finger. Soon the strangeness turned to pleasure.

He didn't know how many fingers Sagami had inside him, but the sensation running through Tatsurou's body made him throw back his head.

Perfect!

It was the same spot Sagami had hit his penis with last time. Tatsurou couldn't help but feel pleasure. Each time Sagami stroked that spot, it felt like an electric shock.

"Ngh…ah!"

Now Sagami's fingers rubbed him gently. The walls of Tatsurou's passage contracted. His body shook from waves of pleasure, while all of his muscles tensed.

While Sagami pushed his fingers in and out, Tatsurou let out a low groan. All of the pleasure he felt was at the whim of Sagami's fingers.

How does he do it?

His arms and knees pinned down, Tatsurou still couldn't move, not that he wanted to escape right now.

"Ngh, ah, mmmmmm…oooh."

Sagami's delicately moving fingers were driving Tatsurou wild. He suddenly noticed he was moving his hips in rhythm to them.

"Tatsurou," Sagami whispered. Each time he moved his fingers, Tatsurou gripped them tight. "How are you're going to make money now?"

"I…don't…know…ah."

Tatsurou couldn't answer questions now. His brain just wouldn't work.

As his lips trembled, Sagami pressed his own on top of them. Making space between the lips, Sagami pushed his tongue deeply inside Tatsurou's mouth. It tasted so sweet, Tatsurou thought that his brain would go numb. As they swapped saliva, Tatsurou lusted for Sagami more and more. All the hair on his body stood up.

Why did this feel so good with Sagami? Being tied up like this, having his body abused. He was chained up like a wild animal, but he still shivered with excitement.

"If you don't pay me in cash, you'll have to pay with your body," Sagami said, pulling away from the kiss.

Tatsurou had lost his Yakuza job, along with his income. But for some strange reason, he still felt everything would be all right in the end. He never, ever wanted to admit his desire for Sagami, but doing this once a month might not be that bad.

"You don't have to pay me with money," Sagami said, removing his fingers.

Almost instantly he replaced them with his hard cock. Tatsurou took a deep breath as Sagami gripped his muscular thighs.

"Today, I won't be gentle. Bad boys like you need to be punished," Sagami teased, his eyes sparkling. He looked so beautiful right now.

"You owe me, so I'll do with you what I like," Sagami went on. "I'm just collecting payment, but consider it a kind of love."

"Wha…!" Tatsurou gasped.

Sagami thrust deep inside him.

As a sharp feeling spread over his body, Tatsurou moaned. "Ah! Ahhh." He almost stopped breathing, but Sagami gently pushed in even further.

"I can get in even deeper than last time, Tatsurou," Sagami crooned. "All the way in."

Tatsurou shook with frustration.

Now Sagami's entire penis was inside him. Sagami didn't even wait for Tatsurou to get used to it, but started moving gently.

"Ngh…oh…"

Each time Sagami's member pushed in, Tatsurou had a strange sensation. Being shafted like this numbed his brain. His pulse was racing now.

Sagami pushed his knees under Tatsurou, lifting up his hips.

"Ugh!"

Sagami moved in even closer and deeper. Now that the position of Sagami's penis had changed, Tatsurou could take it more comfortably. He raised his buttocks a little.

He felt the tip of Sagami's penis deep inside him. If they were going to keep going, he would have to help. He moved his hips up and down, in perfect time with Sagami's thrusts. At first it was difficult to move, but each time he did, the feeling got better. He could never stop now.

"Mmm, ah, ah, AH."

All he could see was white. Ecstasy.

I don't understand, but...

Why did Sagami still like him? He knew Tatsurou couldn't pay the money back, since he'd been fired from his job. What kind of job could he even do now, after being involved with the Yakuza?

...But things aren't bad.

The pleasure shot up his spinal cord to his brain.

The deep thrusting was akin to being swallowed up by a wave.

Lost in this world of pleasure, Tatsurou felt he was becoming a changed man. He could feel himself reaching a quiet place, a place where he could breathe again.

"Tatsurou."

The wave came, consuming his entire body, washing everything away. Just then, he heard Sagami whisper something.

"I love you."

You gotta be kidding.

END

Sleeping With Money

The full-length mirror reflected a young man in a white suit and crimson shirt, which was left open at the neck to show off a large gold medallion.

The young man pushed back his hair and looked at himself. Attractive, yes, but he certainly didn't look law-abiding. Tatsurou Yamamoto smiled grimly.

He pulled a cashmere jacket over his shoulders, wrapped a vermilion scarf around his neck, and completed the look with a brand-new pair of shiny white shoes. Then he posed in the mirror once more.

He put one finger to his chin and the other hand in his coat pocket. This was his arrogant pose. Then he lowered his jaw and glared at his reflection. That was his intimidating pose.

That's it.

Perfect.

He looked menacing enough to frighten a child in the street, the exact effect he was aiming for. Just as he was about to leave and face the world, an approving voice shouted behind him, "Sir, you're looking great!"

Tatsurou turned around. Hachi stood gaping in amazement, his face flushed. When Tatsurou was excommunicated from the Kantou Hinodegumi, he had tried to get rid of Hachi. But Hachi had flat-out refused and now they lived together.

Tatsurou's ten-year-old apartment had two bedrooms, a dining room, and a kitchen. It had looked pretty shabby until Hachi fixed it up after he moved in.

After being initiated with the ceremonial sharing of sake at a young age, Tatsurou had risen to a high position in his Yakuza gang. But three months ago, he had been excommunicated, kicked out of the Yakuza world.

Once your ties had been cut, there was no way you could apply to another Yakuza group. Word got around, though the Yakuza were now so desperate for new members, they might take someone back without question.

But Tatsurou wanted to live an honest life, so cutting ties with the Yakuza had been a good thing. The biggest problem now was his lack of "normal" job experience. He only knew the criminal underworld, and now he'd been pushed into the life of an ordinary working man. Yoshiaki Sagami had even offered him a job at Lovely, one of Japan's top 10 companies, but Tatsurou had flat-out refused.

Tatsurou still had a debt with Sagami to the tune of six million. He now made money collecting on bad debts for Lovely and taking a commission of five percent, just like he did in the Yakuza.

He no longer had his gang's backing to do this job, but that wasn't necessary, since he mostly dealt with law-abiding people. A few gentle threats with his well-trained Yakuza drawl was usually enough for people to quickly cough up the money. When that didn't work, he collected the money by force. His new job was pretty much the same as his old job, but since he was no longer tied to gangs, he could work at his own pace. It wasn't too bad, really.

The only problem is, Sagami keeps begging me to accept an official position in the company.

Tatsurou had gradually warmed up to Sagami and his other co-workers. But he still wasn't sure if he wanted to be Sagami's official employee.

He'd been a Yakuza for so long, he wasn't even sure what else he could do. If he worked directly for Sagami, then Sagami would have even more power over him. Tatsurou didn't want that. Everything he did now was exactly what Sagami desired. His work and personal life were all dictated by Sagami.

I want to be on an equal footing with him.

Leaving the criminal world was hard. It was all he had known for years. He couldn't just become some obedient pet, wagging his tail when his master called.

"I look good?" Tatsurou asked Hachi.

He jammed his hands into his pockets and lifted his head. No doubt about it, his sense of style was still very much Yakuza. Dressing this way was more effective for collecting debts, and also made Tatsurou feel comfortable. He was not ready for a gray salaryman's suit just yet.

I wouldn't mind wearing something like Sagami's though.

Tatsurou's mind painted a picture of Sagami in his expensive, branded garments. You didn't need to see the tag to know that Sagami's fine British suits were top of the line.

"You look really good! Going on a date?" Hachi asked cheerfully.

"A date?" Tatsurou frowned, startled by Hachi's words.

He was actually headed to the Lovely Kantou branch office to repay his debt to Sagami. But in some twisted sense of the word, it might be considered a "date." He eyed Hachi with suspicion.

"Don't get mad, boss!" Hachi begged. "But you're all dressed up and looking excited, just like when you dated those fine bitches."

"Fine bitches? Don't say shit like that," Tatsurou said gruffly, hitting Hachi over the head. He turned around and strode out the door.

With his coat flapping in the wind, Tatsurou headed out into the night. Pedestrians coming the other way stepped aside to avoid the tough-looking man.

Tatsurou felt upset that Hachi had noticed how happy he seemed to go out to repay his debt.

Dammit!

Why did Hachi have to sound so obvious? Now Tatsurou was really fuming.

Why the fuck would I be excited?

Spurred on by rage, Tatsurou quickened his pace.

The sight of Sagami's smooth fingers counting bills was so beautiful it almost looked like art.

"95? You're short 50,000."

"Oh," Tatsurou said dully, leaning back on the

sofa with his legs spread wide.

They were in the office of Lovely's Kantou branch manager. The fluorescent ceiling lights bathed them in a cold white glow. Today was no-overtime day, and since it was after nine o'clock, the other employees had left already.

Tatsurou's heart was racing.

Should I have borrowed the other 50,000 from Hachi?

A loan from Hachi might have been a good idea, since Sagami would now drag him off to his apartment. Hachi was actually doing pretty well financially, even though he had asked Tatsurou if he could move in. Selling dirty panties on the Internet was turning into a real cash cow.

Maybe there was another reason Tatsurou didn't bring Sagami the full amount. If he did, there'd be no reason to sleep together. He'd been with Sagami five times already. By now, he was totally used to the idea; hell, he even enjoyed it. But he didn't go quietly to Sagami's bed. He still put up some token resistance.

Yeah, he forces me. Always been that way, always will be. I only let him take me because I owe him money. That's all, end of story.

Tatsurou had to make these excuses to himself. He still had his male pride, after all. As far as he was concerned, letting a man fuck him was an ordeal, pure and simple.

He always felt tense before they got down to business. His face turned pale and his muscles stiffened.

Sagami smoothly removed 15 bills from the pile. His fingers made a beautiful curve in the air.

"Here, take it," he said. "You need to live, after all. I'll take 80,000 this month."

"O-okay," Tatsurou stuttered.

Each time he made a payment, Sagami gave him back some cash to live on. He was grateful for that, and awkwardly stuffed the bills in his pocket.

Even if he paid the full amount, Sagami would still probably make a deduction, forcing Tatsurou into bed with him. Tatsurou fell deeper into Sagami's trap with each passing day.

"Well then, you'll have to make up the difference with your body again," Sagami said quietly, loosening his tie with one hand. His almond eyes sparkled.

He definitely looked his best when he was in the office. Perfect features, flawless body, the demeanor of an aristocrat. Even his voice sounded different, changing to one that was used to giving orders.

Suddenly, he lost his business persona and became the man he was in private. Tatsurou saw a glint of animal lust in his eyes.

"You wanna do it here?" Tatsurou asked with surprise.

Usually they went to Sagami's apartment.

"Maybe. Is that a problem?" Sagami asked, smiling boldly. Tatsurou knew that no matter what he said, Sagami would not grant him mercy.

Of course it's a problem!

Even though no one was around, it was still an office. Large amounts of cash were kept here, with guards at the entrance. If someone discovered them, there could be real problems for Sagami.

But Sagami doesn't care. Danger actually turns him on.

Tatsurou took a few deep breaths. Resigned to his fate, he extended his hands toward Sagami.

"Tie me up then," he said.

"You actually *like* that?" Sagami asked with surprise.

"I'll hit you if you don't, okay?" Tatsurou replied.

Besides, if he was tied up, then it felt like Sagami was forcing him, or so he told himself.

Sagami smiled gently, seeming to read Tatsurou's thoughts.

"Understood," he said curtly, pulling some rope from his bag.

It's just easier this way.

Some small part of Tatsurou really liked their relationship, though he'd never admit it. Doing it this way—tied up—helped him keep up the pretense. He had no intention of changing things now. Maybe he never would.

Tatsurou took off his white blazer, leaving only his crimson shirt. Sagami tied Tatsurou's wrists securely behind his back, then wrapped the rest of the rope around his arms and chest, making it difficult for Tatsurou to breathe.

"Ngh."

Tatsurou had never gotten used to this heady feeling of anticipation. He glanced at himself in the tinted windows, then quickly averted his eyes. Seeing himself tied up like this was just too much. Sagami noticed and pulled down the blinds.

Tatsurou shivered as he watched Sagami move.

It's throbbing.

Under the silk shirt, he felt the rope rub his nipples. Sagami always teased Tatsurou's ultra-sensitive nipples to entice him into sex. The friction of the rope stimulated them. Soon two little knobs popped out from under the shirt. Sagami wrapped his arms around Tatsurou from behind.

"Ah!" Tatsurou squeaked.

Being tied up like this had put him on edge. As soon as Sagami touched him, Tatsurou's body quivered. It was a tense feeling, like electric shocks coursing through his muscles.

"A month is a long time, don't you think?" Sagami said idly, twiddling Tatsurou's nipples between his fingers. That alone was enough to make Tatsurou groan. His head spun with sexual desire. He had felt this way before, but in the days and weeks between their encounters, he always forgot how good it felt.

"Wouldn't it be nice to get together more often?" Sagami suggested. "These long dry spells must be difficult for such a sensitive body like yours."

Sagami plunged his hand under Tatsurou's shirt, flicking the nipples between his fingertips. Tatsurou quivered at the sensation, trying not to groan too loud. He was quickly getting aroused. Sagami knew exactly where to touch him.

"Yeah, like hell!" Tatsurou began but lost his

train of thought. "I…ooh…ah."

Now Sagami was nibbling his earlobe. Tatsurou's shoulders dropped. Sagami loosened Tatsurou's belt and shoved his hand down his pants.

As Sagami's hands fondled him all over, Tatsurou got more and more turned on. Having Sagami touch him this way felt so different from normal touching. Deep inside his heart, Tatsurou knew he wanted Sagami.

"A month is a long time," Sagami moaned. "I wanted you. I dreamed about fucking you every single day."

He pushed Tatsurou against the wall, his hand covered in lubricant.

"Oh…" Tatsurou moaned.

Sagami pushed his slippery finger inside Tatsurou. It had been a whole month now, so he felt tight. As Sagami pushed his whole finger inside, Tatsurou's breathing became labored. His body remembered what it felt like to be touched there. His frequent, desperate gasps sounded like he was having an asthma attack.

Sagami gently pulled out and pushed back in, while Tatsurou's muscles spasmed with each thrust. His entire body went numb. Even his knees were shaking. He wanted Sagami to move his finger inside him more urgently. But as soon as his body got used to the feeling, he got impatient.

He wanted to feel much more than this. He wanted Sagami to probe even deeper, so he started to move his hips.

"Tatsurou…are you liking this?" Sagami asked.

"Of course not! Take it out!" Tatsurou hissed,

turning bright red. Sagami started to pull his finger out, but Tatsurou's muscles gripped it tightly, trying to stop Sagami's escape.

"I, uh, actually didn't mean it..." Tatsurou said sheepishly.

Sagami laughed.

Bastard!

Tatsurou glared over his shoulder at Sagami, his cloudy eyes unable to focus. Sagami thrust more fingers into him, with even more force. Tatsurou groaned with pleasure. He was pinned against the wall, his bound hands clenched into fists.

As he tried to relax his muscles, giving Sagami's fingers better access, Tatsurou felt that strange tingly sensation again.

Sagami's fingers twisted and turned, exploring the depths inside him. Tatsurou became totally lost in the moment, moving his hips against Sagami's fingers. He couldn't stop himself. Soon they were moving in perfect rhythm. Tatsurou let himself go, indulging his carnal lust.

But as good as it felt, Sagami's big cock inside him would feel even better.

"My! What a dirty little boy!" Sagami teased, quickly pushing his fingers in and out.

Tatsurou felt that strange heat rising in his body, threatening to consume every part of him. He was ashamed that he enjoyed disgracing his body like this, but the humiliation made it all the more stimulating.

"Ngh...please..." he begged, his cheek pressed against the wall. His face looked flushed, his

mouth wide open in ecstasy.

Sagami pulled him closer for a kiss.

"You want me to enter you now?" he asked. "But it'll hurt if you're not warmed up a little more."

He pushed Tatsurou up against the wall, so his body would be well supported. Then he skillfully twisted his fingers inside Tatsurou, hitting all the right places. He also sped up the pace. Now he had three fingers inside Tatsurou, moving them in and out, in and out, over and over and over again.

Every thrust made Tatsurou clench his teeth. The lubricant made dirty squishing sounds, which made him feel even more embarrassed. He tightened the muscles in his ass, trying to stop the nasty sound, but found it just excited him more.

Try as he might, he couldn't stop his legs from collapsing under him. Sagami kept pulling him back up. But under Sagami's skilled touch, standing was just not possible.

"Put it in," Tatsurou moaned. It almost sounded like a sob.

"Are you going to come?" Sagami asked.

"Just do it, jerk…" Tatsurou panted.

At Tatsurou's insult, Sagami finally took out his fingers. Tatsurou was having too much trouble standing at this point, so Sagami led him over to his shiny desk.

The desk held only a computer, a pencil holder, and two trays marked "in" and "out." There was plenty of room for Sagami to spread out Tatsurou's body.

"Ah," Tatsurou shivered as he felt something cold between his buttocks. Sagami was basting him with lubricant.

Tatsurou had the usual mixed feelings as he waited for Sagami to enter him. He pushed his cheek against the desk, resigned to his fate.

"I'm going in. Loosen up," Sagami said in a pleading tone.

Tatsurou felt the warm tip of Sagami's member push between his buttocks. His body trembled with excitement as he felt the hot stiff cock.

"Ah!" he gasped.

Bit by bit, the hard foreign object pushed its way inside him. The pain only lasted for a moment, though. Within seconds, the head of Sagami's penis was fully inside. Tatsurou let out a great gasp. He was doing his best to relax his body, but Sagami could never push his whole cock inside if Tatsurou was this tight.

Sagami lay on top of Tatsurou, wrapping his arms around Tatsurou's waist. The rope still rubbed against Tatsurou's nipples, creating little stabs of pleasure. Sagami pinched them even harder, sending a wave of pleasure surging throughout his body.

"Uh," Tatsurou grunted. He shifted position, accidentally forcing Sagami's penis in even deeper. He gasped in pain. "Fuck! Not so fast…"

"Me? You were the one who did it," Sagami snorted, pinching Tatsurou's nipples.

Tatsurou couldn't hold back. He wanted to feel Sagami inside him more than he ever dreamed possible. But Sagami had stopped thrusting to fondle Tatsurou's nipples, already rock hard from rubbing against the rope. Now the slightest touch made Tatsurou swoon with pleasure.

"You really are sensitive here, you know?" Sagami observed, opening Tatsurou's shirt to expose his nipples. Tatsurou felt dizzy as he glanced down to see what Sagami was doing.

This is…a turn on…!

He saw the rope digging into his crimson shirt as Sagami gently massaged his hard pink nipples. Now Tatsurou felt a stirring in his crotch. Just the tip of Sagami was inside him now. He encouraged the sensation by swaying from side to side, so Sagami's penis would touch more of him.

"Oh…mmmm…"

The tip of Sagami's tongue caressed his ear, making Tatsurou's hips sway even more desperately. He wanted more. He needed more. His body burned with desire. He contracted the muscles in his ass, inviting Sagami to push in deeper.

Finally Sagami took the lead. Each time Sagami moved, Tatsurou let out a little groan. Each time, he didn't think he would last much longer. Sagami gave Tatsurou just the head of his penis though and pinched even harder on his nipples. Tatsurou was almost crying with frustration now. He needed Sagami inside him. He couldn't stand it anymore.

He slowly pushed back his ass, eager to have Sagami probe him more deeply.

"Tatsurou, you're so cute. Is this what you want?"

Shit.

Tatsurou blushed bright red, embarrassed that Sagami noticed his desire. Seeing Tatsurou blush seemed to make Sagami give in. He finally gave Tatsurou what he wanted, thrusting into him deep and hard.

"AH!"

Sagami's hard member was inside him now. It was such painful, painful pleasure.

In that moment, Tatsurou felt complete. He gasped and his muscles tensed. Slowly, Sagami moved inside him. Tatsurou felt a little pain, but mostly overwhelming pleasure. Sagami kept on teasing him, pulling back until he was almost out, then pushing hard back inside. Tatsurou groaned with each thrust.

"Oh…ah…mmmmmm…ah."

The more of Sagami he took, the more he loosened up. With every inward thrust, Tatsurou felt more and more relaxed. Every time Sagami pulled out, Tatsurou tensed his muscles. They were in perfect rhythm with each other.

It took supreme effort on Tatsurou's part to hold himself back. Just when he thought he couldn't take any more, his greedy body wouldn't let him stop.

Sagami just kept thrusting at him. Finally he whispered, "I love being inside you. You drain me dry."

"What…stupid…ah," Tatsurou groaned.

His mind went blank. He tried everything to stop himself.

Sagami kissed him gently and whispered in his ear, "I can make you come if you want."

He grabbed Tatsurou's penis and stroked its moist head. This unfamiliar sensation made Tatsurou lean backward, which only pushed his ass further onto Sagami's hard cock. One of his nipples was still being tweaked and he was being shafted hard from behind.

"Aaaaah!"

Tatsurou's whole body tensed up, straining the ropes still tied around him. His crotch shook. His penis suddenly erupted, then went completely limp, like it would never rise again.

With a long gasp, he finally relaxed, but Sagami was still inside him.

"Ngh…" Tatsurou groaned again.

Sagami climbed on the desk. With his legs on each side of Tatsurou, he pushed deeper.

"I…hate…you…" Tatsurou moaned.

He needed a break, but he had to admit that his body was still burning for more.

Later, they went back to Sagami's place, where they spent a very passionate night.

Finally, Tatsurou fell asleep, totally worn out. When he opened his eyes, the sun was already up. Still exhausted from the night before, he craved for more sleep. But when he noticed Sagami watching him, he suddenly didn't feel drowsy anymore. He lifted his aching body and staggered into the bathroom, checking his watch. It was already noon. And today was Saturday, Sagami's day off.

Fucking hell.

He filled the bathtub and sunk his body into the warm water, staring up at the white tiled ceiling.

Do I really have to do these disgusting things?

His body had been covered with sweat and other

bodily fluids, but Sagami must have wiped him off last night. Tatsurou had some vague memory of it.

As he got out of the tub and dried himself off, he wondered how he should treat Sagami the morning after.

I don't really dislike him.

But Tatsurou had no idea how to actually be fond of someone. Being so submissive felt weird to him. He hated the lack of control.

When Sagami had saved him from the fire, Tatsurou agreed they could date. But *only* date.

It's only my body. Just my body.

He brushed his hair away from his face. Touching his finger to his forehead, he let out a long sigh.

It felt good when Sagami took him. He still wasn't sure how he felt about sex with men, but maybe he could lose all of his hang-ups.

And then...

He wiped his lips on his arm.

When I'm with him, I feel good...

Tatsurou was from a very dysfunctional family. All he had known since childhood was struggle, struggle, struggle. But for some reason, Sagami had a strange way of calming him down. He felt so comfortable around Sagami it almost sickened him. Whenever he was frustrated, Sagami was always there. He had never known anyone like this man before, but he still felt really confused.

Fuck. I can't start liking the guy...

He sighed again, his body remembering every part Sagami had touched with his hands or his lips.

He shivered a little. His body didn't feel like his own anymore. But it was hard to let your guard down after so many years.

Giving his body was one thing, but giving his heart was entirely different. Even so, a tiny piece of it already belonged to Sagami.

He would never sleep with a guy he didn't like, at least a little.

"Hey, Sagami! Where're my clothes…"

Tatsurou went back to the living room wearing only a bathrobe. He still felt tired, but his head had cleared. His stomach made hungry noises. Maybe they could go out for lunch together.

Sagami's apartment building was very different from Tatsurou's. Every floor had staff on duty 24/7, making it seem much less lonely.

Sagami grabbed Tatsurou as soon as he entered the living room. He sat him on the sofa and wrapped his hair in a dry towel.

"Huh?" Tatsurou grunted.

"You should dry it," Sagami scolded gently, rubbing Tatsurou's wet hair.

Having his hair touched by another person felt nice. Tatsurou closed his eyes and enjoyed the sensation.

Sagami looked at him closely. "Never let another man see you this defenseless."

"What the fuck are you talking about now?" Tatsurou growled.

They were starting to feel like real lovers.

Sagami blotted off the excess water, then fluffed Tatsurou's hair with a blow-dryer. Tatsurou liked being touched like this. It was relaxing. Sex was good, but this made him feel warm inside. When his hair was dry, he got up from the sofa.

"Where are my clothes?" he asked again.

"In the laundry," Sagami replied. "I have other clothes you can wear, though."

Tatsurou looked blank. "Huh?"

"You always look good, trust me. But maybe you'd like to try a new style?" Sagami suggested, grabbing a box from the corner of the room.

The name of an upscale store was printed on top. It definitely didn't look cheap. Tatsurou's heart beat a little faster as Sagami pulled out a three-piece suit.

"A *real* suit?" Tatsurou murmured with amazement. The suit was elegantly tailored, made from the finest British fabric. It was the same style that Sagami always wore.

Sagami held the suit as he gently nagged, "Will you wear it? I took measurements while you were asleep. It's tailor-made, so it should fit you perfectly."

"Ah." Tatsurou nodded.

He didn't know what to say. The suit must have cost at least several hundred thousand yen. He wanted to take it, but hesitated. Sagami knew Tatsurou could never return the favor.

"When a guy gives another guy clothes, it's just to see him naked," Tatsurou blabbered. "Or so I've heard."

"Oh?" Sagami said mildly.

Tatsurou looked at Sagami and laughed, knowing that seeing him naked was not nearly enough.

"Why don't you work for Lovely? I've asked you three times now. I can sort things out for you," Sagami proposed.

"A regular suit, a regular job?" Tatsurou mused.

He grimaced at the very idea. But if he could wear a suit like this every day, maybe it wouldn't be so bad. To his amazement, Sagami quickly pulled out new shoes, new socks, and new boxer shorts.

After Tatsurou donned the suit, Sagami carefully tied his tie for him, then turned him to inspect his reflection in the mirror.

"Add a spritz of fine cologne, and you'll be just like a millionaire's son," Sagami whispered, making Tatsurou shiver a little.

Sagami was the son of a rich man, surrounded by luxuries since birth. He definitely knew how to dress the part, not a single hair was ever out of place on him. Tatsurou agreed that Sagami did have class.

This made Tatsurou feel inferior, maybe even a little jealous. He turned back to the mirror to hide the expression on his face. But there he was, looking as dignified and high-class as Sagami.

The well-made suit complimented Tatsurou's lanky frame. Even his wrinkles looked alluring, and his glare didn't seem menacing anymore. In fact, he looked exactly like a law-abiding man.

Oooo.

All of a sudden, Tatsurou felt something inside

him stir. Could just this change in appearance actually change his life? Maybe he really could live an honest life.

Sagami stepped up to help him into the long coat, then wrapped a cashmere scarf around his neck.

"You are so beautiful," Sagami whispered in awe. "I just might fall in love with you. Shall we go for lunch? I made a reservation."

Now Tatsurou felt like an escort.

"All right," he agreed.

He smiled. He could see the mirror image of himself happily smiling back.

This is how honest people live and work. The idea totally excited him.

The restaurant Sagami had selected required formal attire only. A doorman hurried to open the door as they approached. Tatsurou felt a bit nervous, but he didn't really need to be. All he had to do was copy what Sagami did. They left their coats with the cloakroom attendant, then were shown to a private room.

The high-class cuisine astounded Tatsurou with their exquisite flavors. He gobbled down everything in sight, filling his empty stomach.

Sagami always took him to great restaurants, but, somehow, today seemed special. As they waited for dessert, Tatsurou asked Sagami a frank question.

"What's the matter with you today?"

Something was definitely up today—the classy restaurant, the expensive suit. Sagami had spent a small fortune on him, but why?

Sagami smiled demurely, in a manner befitting the expensive surroundings.

"Today is February 14th," he beamed.

"Well, don't expect any chocolate, okay? I don't do things like that," Tatsurou grumbled.

No way in hell would he do such a thing, but Sagami didn't seem disappointed. Instead, he looked a little surprised.

"That's fine. But don't you remember something else about this day?" he asked.

"Huh? February 14th?" Tatsurou muttered.

Just then, the waiter carefully placed a beautiful dessert in front of Tatsurou. The lights dimmed as the waiter soaked the cake with brandy and lit a match. A crown of blue flames burst up.

"Happy Birthday," Sagami whispered.

Tatsurou watched the flames burn until they went out and the lights came back on.

Birthday?

"Oh," he said.

He had completely forgotten. His family never celebrated birthdays. Instead, his mother usually cursed that she had ever given birth to him in the first place. He was at a complete loss for words.

Smiling, Sagami pulled out a beautifully-wrapped box.

"Here's your present," he said.

"Wasn't the suit enough?" Tatsurou said. "You're giving me more?"

Sagami kept smiling.

"Open it," he said.

Tatsurou obediently did as told. The waiter quickly served them coffee and left them alone.

Inside the larger box was a small box marked "Rolex." Tatsurou's heart thumped as he opened it. Inside was an Oyster Perpetual Day-Date watch.

Whoa!

Ten small diamonds glittered around the cool blue watch face. It was gorgeous, the king of Rolex watches, a real status symbol. So beautiful, it almost took Tatsurou's breath away.

"I…" he stuttered, grasping for words. Was this really a present? But it was worth nearly eight million yen!

He had admired this same watch on Sagami a while back, and actually sent Hachi for a Rolex catalog. But after checking out the price, he had quickly given up his dream of actually owning one.

"A perfect match." Sagami lifted his sleeve to show Tatsurou his watch.

"Huh?" Tatsurou gasped, his pupils dilating. So now they had matching watches, just like a couple in love.

He was elated to have something he had wanted so badly. Though one might question Sagami's spending habits, as far as Tatsurou was concerned, he was just happy to receive something so wonderful. True, being together still felt a bit awkward and embarrassing, but he was very thankful for Sagami's gifts.

"Thank you," he said gruffly.

Sagami smiled broadly. "You're welcome."

"How did you know I wanted this? Did Hachi tell you?" Tatsurou asked.

"Yep," Sagami replied. "Hachi is an excellent source of information. I hear he's living at your place now?"

"Only because he asked to, but it's starting to get a little annoying," Tatsurou grumbled.

Unlike Tatsurou, Hachi had never taken part in the sake-sharing ceremony. He could go anywhere, but refused to leave Tatsurou's side. He also did all the housework, so Tatsurou really couldn't complain much.

"By the way, have you noticed that I'm now Lovely's Kantou Branch Manager?" Sagami asked between sips of coffee.

Tatsurou's eyes popped wide open. He hadn't noticed.

Lovely had grown rapidly in recent years, riding the tail of the quick-loan boom. There were now 1,500 branches across the country. He remembered seeing this number on a poster inside the Kantou Branch.

The Kantou area included a few hundred branches, and now Sagami was at the top of the heap.

"Wow," Tatsurou whistled. "And you're only 27, like me. Guess your family really is wealthy."

"The branch manager has a lot of authority. The first one designed the company that way," Sagami said, taking out a gold business card holder and passing it to Tatsurou.

Tatsurou assumed it held Sagami's new business cards, but the cards inside read "Lovely (Ltd.) Kantou Branch, Assistant to the Branch Manager, Yamamoto Tatsurou."

Tatsurou felt pleased but, at the same time, not. He didn't like being asked to totally abandon his freedom.

"Is this some kind of joke? I never agreed to work for you," he griped in a low tone.

But this didn't work on Sagami, who returned Tatsurou's menacing look with a smile.

"I thought about talking you into it before I gave them to you," he said. "I knew you have no job plans at the moment. And it would be nice to have you all to myself."

Sagami's methods were a mystery to Tatsurou. If Tatsurou didn't watch out, he'd always be Sagami's underling. He started to throw the business cards back to Sagami's face.

"That's solid gold," Sagami said calmly.

"Ngh," Tatsurou grunted, stopping himself.

He couldn't treat something of value like that. He'd been broke for just too long.

"Please just take them. You don't have to use them," Sagami whispered.

"I'll take them, but I don't know if I'll use them," Tatsurou said reluctantly, tucking the cards into his chest pocket.

An honest man's suit. An honest man's business cards.

Tatsurou was gradually undergoing a complete transformation—yet for some reason, he felt happy.

But he still couldn't admit it to himself.

A few days later, Tatsurou cheerfully put on his new suit and headed to Lovely's Kantou branch office.

He was still a debt collector. In the past, wearing a Yakuza suit automatically made people give their money to him. Now, it didn't really matter. Tatsurou had so much experience, he easily collected most debts no matter what he was wearing.

Besides, the new suit made him feel good.

Now, pedestrians didn't nervously move out of his way, and high school girls often commented on his good looks. He really enjoyed this new sense of well being.

This time, the company with a debt was called Heart System. Lovely's previous branch manager had arranged the loan, three hundred million of outstanding debt which really stressed out Sagami. They had pushed Heart System to sell their real estate, but now another company was making claims on the company's assets.

"Well, try to make sense of the situation and collect as much as you can," Sagami told Tatsurou.

Suddenly, the phone on his desk rang. Sagami picked it up, signaling Tatsurou to wait a minute. Tatsurou sipped coffee the secretary had given him and looked around the large room.

He'd been here many times before. There was the impressive large desk and a luxurious sofa. Everything suited Sagami's expensive taste.

Assistant to the Branch Manager. Does that mean I'd work in here?

Sagami's voice suddenly interrupted Tatsurou's thoughts.

He's speaking English?

Sagami was talking to someone in perfect English. Now he was even laughing, like they had just shared a joke. He sounded completely at ease.

That's amazing.

Tatsurou was impressed. He knew Sagami was smart, but this completely blew him away.

After Sagami agreed to another meeting, the conversation came to an end. He hung up the phone and turned back to Tatsurou.

"Sorry I made you wait," he said.

"No problem. You speak English, eh?" Tatsurou said with admiration.

Sagami just shrugged. "Not very fluently, just enough to do business. You haven't been abroad much, have you? The week after next, I'm off to Europe. Why don't you come too? While I attend boring business meetings, you can go sightseeing."

"What kind of boring business meetings?" Tatsurou asked.

"We have some spare capital, but there are no attractive investment opportunities in Japan right now," Sagami explained. "We're creating an overseas fund, so I'll be meeting with investors about that."

Spare capital?

The concept of extra money was completely foreign to Tatsurou. He took another sip of the superb coffee and frowned.

"I don't have a passport," he admitted.

"Get one," Sagami said. "There should be time before we leave."

Another phone call came in. Now Sagami spoke in Japanese. "Yes, he's taking care of it. The funds for this election? Yes. Please let him continue."

Must be a politician, Tatsurou thought.

Probably a parliamentary representative, since they were talking about the general election. Tatsurou took a cookie from a plate on the desk and nibbled on it. Sagami was using a soft coaxing voice, just like a corrupt official. He hung up and immediately called one of his employees.

"Yes, the election money," Sagami said. "Fund up to two hundred million with no security needed. By the day after tomorrow. Yes, the review body."

Sagami looked so different when he was working. Tatsurou had never seen him like this before. It seemed that if you wanted to be a branch manager, you had to speak English. You also had to pander to politicians. Tatsurou was absolutely stunned by the huge sums of money being offered.

He stood up and brushed cookie crumbs off his suit. The third phone call seemed to be going on and on, so he decided to go out to make the collection. He waved at Sagami as he left, not wanting to disturb him.

Assistant to the Branch Manager.

Tatsurou's mind was racing as he plodded down the stairs. The manager's office was on the top floor of the four-story building, the first and second floors were devoted to large financial loans. Lovely's employees all seemed quite capable, and Tatsurou could hear managers giving strict orders to them.

His new suit didn't attract as much attention as

the old one. He smiled as he remembered his first visit here, when they had regarded him as some rare beast that might bite at any provocation. Back then, he was quickly ushered into a private reception room.

Tatsurou decided to stop in the employee lounge for a smoke.

Ah.

He puffed on his cigarette and stretched out on the sofa. After seeing hard-charging Sagami at work, he was feeling a bit insecure.

What the hell can I do? he thought, blowing a trail of smoke.

Today, he would collect debts. He was very good at getting people to pay up, but what else could he do? He wanted to believe Sagami had hired him for his skills, not just because he liked him. Real men don't get jobs through their boyfriends.

As he stubbed out his cigarette, he heard voices nearby.

"What the hell does the manager think he's doing, letting Yakuza scum into the office?"

Tatsurou's ears pricked up at the words "Yakuza scum."

"What happens when people find out about him? It'll be a disaster for Lovely's image," someone else said.

"If the papers find out, there'll be a public scandal. I've heard that our president wants to enter politics. But rumors like this will…"

The gossipers were both elderly men. Lovely employed lots of young people, but there were still old workers left from when the company had been called Sagami Financing. Now they were executives.

Tatsurou waited until the two men passed him by before he spoke up.

"You have a problem with me?"

He leaned back on the sofa, legs spread wide, and gave them a cool, defiant look. No matter how nice his suit was, he could still make them shiver with fear.

"Wahh!" one gasped.

"Ah, umm, ummm," stammered the other.

The two old men were so terrified, they dropped the documents in their hands. But Tatsurou quickly lost interest in them, having achieved the desired effect.

"Got something to say to me? Then say it to my face!" he spat out.

Tatsurou thought that would be the end of it. He assumed they would hurry away, unwilling to cause a scene at work.

But one executive shot back at him, trembling with rage, "We...we can't accept having someone like you working for Mr. Yoshiaki. Mr. Yoshiaki should be thinking of this company!"

"Heh," Tatsurou snorted, squinting at them.

MISTER Yoshiaki. They've gotta be kidding.

Tatsurou couldn't believe that other people would even talk about their relationship, let alone have an opinion about it. He got up from the sofa looking livid. The executive gulped. Other employees stopped as they passed by, waiting with baited breath.

Tatsurou wouldn't beat the executive up, just threaten him a little. He did not like to be mocked. As he stepped forward, one executive let out a little scream.

Suddenly a sharp, imposing voice cut through the tension.

"What's going on here?"

Tatsurou turned around to see Sagami. Behind him, Sagami's secretary held his coat and bag. Sagami definitely called the shots here, which was to be expected from the branch manager.

"These bastards said Yakuza scum shouldn't be here," Tatsurou protested. "I was just messing with them a little."

Sagami nodded and turned to the men.

"He has my permission to be here, gentlemen. Tatsurou has proven himself very useful in debt collection. He successfully collected money from the Maruichi Sake Company and the Oohara Product Company, which you had such difficulty in doing. Or have you forgotten?"

"No. We…we just think you shouldn't deal with him directly. Use more appropriate people, instead of Yakuza scum," a man explained.

"So he's Yakuza scum, huh?" Sagami asked.

The executive looked baffled. "Huh? But he is, isn't he?"

"Tatsurou left his gang to work for me," Sagami said coldly. "If anything happens, *I'll* take the blame. The financial world always needs the services of criminals. But I will *not* pretend they have nothing to do with me just to keep my own hands clean. That, gentlemen, is not my style."

Sagami's voice sounded deep and impressive.

He definitely *was* different at work.

"Got any more complaints?" he added.

The executives were at a loss for words. Sagami marched away, motioning for Tatsurou to come with him.

"I'll drop you off at Heart System. I have something to discuss with you," he said.

"Okay, sure…" Tatsurou muttered. He felt slightly miffed that Sagami had jumped in to rescue him. He wanted to look after himself.

Still, he had been vindicated. He followed Sagami with his head held high.

The company car of the Lovely Kantou branch manager was a black Crown Majesta. According to Sagami, the vehicle had cost a cool one hundred million. It had been tricked out with armor plating just like a VIP car.

As soon as they got in, Sagami raised the screen between the driver and passengers.

"Sorry about that," he said quietly.

The coldness he had shown before the executives softened now that he was alone with Tatsurou.

"Don't worry. You don't have to apologize for them." Tatsurou frowned.

Don't you think I can stand up for myself?

"I promise it won't happen again," Sagami said. "My office will *not* become a place you don't feel comfortable in. I want you to have my support."

"But I'm useless to you! I don't speak English.

I mess up business meetings. I can't even make tea," Tatsurou sulked.

"We don't know that yet," Sagami pointed out.

"You haven't realized by now?" Tatsurou grumbled.

Sagami just smiled.

Before Tatsurou had a chance to reply, the car came to a stop. He was opening the door to get out when Sagami grabbed his arm.

"People keep telling me I shouldn't be seeing you. Maybe you've heard them, too. But please ignore them. You're the only one in my heart," Sagami said urgently.

He looked so serious. Tatsurou's heart raced.

"Whatever happens, I'm not letting you go," Sagami continued. "Believe in that."

Sagami didn't need to say it, Tatsurou already knew. Still, hearing it in words made it even more powerful.

Sagami was deeply in love with Tatsurou. That much was obvious.

I'm like a little girl, excited by lovey-dovey stuff.

Tatsurou bolted out of the car so Sagami wouldn't see him blushing.

"Shut the hell up. Don't say that shit. Now go do your work. WORK!" Tatsurou snapped.

Tatsurou entered the main office of Heart System, a trustee corporation that sold food to factories and hospitals. A family-run business, Heart System had managed to keep ahead of the competition for years. Now they were going under because of bad management.

When Tatsurou asked where he could find the manager, they gave him the address of a shabby hotel in a back street.

He went there to talk with the man and learned that Heart System's real estate, used as collateral on the loan, had already been sold to the Seishoukai. The manager trembled with fear as he told Tatsurou about the sale. There was clearly nothing more Tatsurou could get out of this poor man. The only option left was to speak to the Seishoukai.

The Seishoukai.

Tatsurou sighed.

It was a powerful regional gang, even tougher than the Kantou Hinodegumi or the Kantou Asahigumi. The Seishoukai was primarily based in Kansai, but it had stretched its tentacles into Kantou as well.

Yakuza.

Things were getting out of hand. No way could an ex-Yakuza get respect from someone still on the inside. The chances of him getting his point across looked very slim indeed.

To make things worse, Tatsurou had never been on good terms with the Seishoukai. He had always been at odds with Kobayakawa, the president of the Seishoukai Tokyo branch. For some reason, Kobayakawa was always hostile to Tatsurou.

Why?

Tatsurou never knew why Kobayakawa hated

him so much. Kobayakawa had been in Kantou when he was young, then later moved to Kansai. Tatsurou couldn't remember what, if anything, had happened between them, but there must have been something.

The largest Seishoukai office in Tokyo was near Shinjuku. Tatsurou got out of the taxi and smoked a cigarette to calm his nerves.

The building itself looked ordinary. You would never guess that it was the Seishoukai's office from the exterior. But if you actually stepped inside, you'd soon see that the place was just crawling with Yakuza. If anything bad happened, Tatsurou would never escape.

This is not good.

There was no way he could walk into their office, threaten them for money, and walk out with it in his hands.

But I have to talk to them.

If Tatsurou couldn't get the three hundred million, Sagami would be gravely disappointed in him. He wanted to show those executives—and prove to Sagami—that he could do something important.

No fancy British-made suit could cover up the vicious expression on Tatsurou's face. People passing on the street nervously skirted around him.

Well. Let's do this.

Tatsurou stamped out his cigarette and readied himself.

When he was in the Kantou Hinodegumi, he needed permission from the president to act. Now he took orders from no one. The only downside was that he had no back-up for situations like this one, walking straight into the enemy's camp. He wasn't even carrying a knife today.

But pulling a knife could make everything worse.

To Tatsurou, a knife was just another threat, he never actually used it as a weapon. If he was caught brandishing one, he'd get sent to prison.

He stood outside the door and pressed the intercom button. Almost instantly, someone answered, some young punk who manned the entrance. Tatsurou was in no mood to chat with underlings today, and pushed right past him. The poor kid was too shocked to do anything.

Inside, Tatsurou saw a long hallway, plus an office lined with desks. He also recognized two Seishoukai Yakuza he slightly knew from before.

"I need to speak to Kobayakawa about Heart System's debt," he called out.

He squared his shoulders, his hands still thrust in his pockets. The Hinodegumi was a small gang. Though Tatsurou had been a leading member, he no longer had that position. But he didn't want them to know that.

"You're Tatsurou, right? You look different," a guy said, getting out from behind his desk.

It must have been strange for him to see Tatsurou dressed like a rich boy.

The Yakuza looked him up and down. "You're looking damn good, Tatsurou. Been selling your body or something?"

"Shut the fuck up. I asked to speak with Kobayakawa. KOBAYAKAWA!" Tatsurou screamed.

One second later, a stream of black coffee splashed over his head.

Luckily it was cold, but Tatsurou was still stunned for a moment. Evidently, they were totally unafraid of an ex-Yakuza, which made Tatsurou's blood boil.

"Bastard!" he spat out, grabbing the Yakuza by his collar. He gave the man a swift, strong punch, then kicked him over his desk.

The Hinodegumi may have been small potatoes, but they had lots of fighting experience. Victory always came to whoever made the first move. Tatsurou thought more guys would appear, but no one did. He marched out into the corridor to find the young punk looking terrified.

"Where's everybody today? Where's Kobayakawa?" he demanded, grabbing the kid's collar. Suddenly, the door swung open. A fist flew at him from behind. He dodged the attack, but just barely. As another fist pummeled into his stomach, he doubled over in pain. In a fight like this, just one second of hesitation often proved fatal.

"You've got some guts, brat," he hissed.

Through his pain he heard more Yakuza quickly approaching. Unable to defend himself, he turned his back to the wall and kneeled on the floor. Two men grabbed his arms and twisted them back.

"You're Kobayakawa," Tatsurou choked.

Ten henchmen surrounded Kobayakawa, who was as tall as Sagami. He also wore glasses, unusual for a gangster. Tatsurou had heard he was a graduate of Tokyo

University, but the Yakuza world was filled with lies. Either way, Kobayakawa was a modern "intellectual" Yakuza, fairly handsome, but also quite jittery.

"Why did you storm into my office? Explain," Kobayakawa asked quietly, pushing his glasses up his nose.

Tatsurou felt instantly overwhelmed. This man could unleash the entire Seishoukai Tokyo branch on him with a single word. Coming here without back-up had been way too reckless, and now Tatsurou was terrified. If he'd been a regular guy, the Yakuza wouldn't touch him. But he was ex-Yakuza, which meant they could beat him to a pulp without fear of police retaliation.

Tatsurou, still kneeling on the ground, defiantly raised his chin. If he let this man mock him, it would definitely be all over. Fixing his eyes on Kobayakawa, he stated his reason for being there.

"I'm here about Heart System's debt. You sold what Lovely had marked as collateral."

"So you're here for a piece of the action, eh? Sorry, it's first come, first served," Kobayakawa sneered.

"Don't give me that bullshit!" Tatsurou growled.

The Yakuza on his left and the Yakuza on his right both punched him hard in the gut. He lost consciousness. When he came to, his head was hanging inches from the floor.

Kobayakawa strode towards him and said, "Sorry, Tatsurou, I had no choice but to beat you up. I can't have people insulting me."

The trademark Yakuza growl was familiar music to Tatsurou's ears. But why this was all happening, he didn't understand.

Bastard!

No matter how hard he tried to defend himself, the punches pinned him down so he could barely move.

Kobayakawa leaned over to grab something shiny off the floor, the business card holder Sagami had given him.

"Pretty fancy deal you got here," Kobayakawa remarked.

"GIVE IT BACK!" Tatsurou screamed.

Kobayakawa opened it and took out a card.

"Lovely, Kantou Branch, Assistant to the Branch Manager, Tatsurou Yamamoto. So! The Hinodegumi kicked you out, and now you work at Lovely," Kobayakawa said viciously. "You must be *really* close to the branch manager, that one who's gonna be president."

Suddenly Kobayakawa smiled.

Does he know about us?

Did Kobayakawa know about him and Sagami? Tatsurou had a bad feeling about this.

Kobayakawa glared at Tatsurou, still hanging inches from the floor.

"You may be assistant to the branch manager, but you haven't changed one bit," he muttered. "Since when does an honest Lovely employee start a brawl here? You can't have worked there for very long. What if we call the police? I can see the headlines now! 'Lovely employee, ex-gang member, charged with assault.' 'Lovely suspected of criminal activity.' This won't be just your problem. All of your Lovely friends will be in trouble. I heard your profits rose after that kitty commercial. But what will happen now?"

"Shut the fuck up. Cut the bullshit, Kobayakawa," Tatsurou growled.

Tatsurou talked a good game, but he knew he was in big trouble.

Sagami will go down with me…

That damn business card! Now Lovely itself was at risk. If there was a lawsuit, Sagami would have to be involved. Tatsurou hated to think that Sagami could take the blame for his foolishness.

They'll extort all his money.

Sometimes, gangs blackmailed companies beset with scandals that would wreck their image if made public. Tatsurou hated himself for setting up Lovely like this.

"You guys will look bad, too!" Tatsurou insisted. "You'll be a laughingstock for beating up a regular guy!"

"Who gives a damn? I could care less about my image," Kobayakawa scoffed.

"Give me back the cards!" Tatsurou yelled.

"Not without an apology, Tatsurou," Kobayakawa retorted. "Throw yourself on the ground and say you're sorry."

He looked Tatsurou over, like a snake sizing up its prey. He wouldn't let Tatsurou go, not just yet.

Like hell I'll kneel on the ground, Tatsurou thought, gritting his teeth.

He was too proud for that, but he had another problem. If he didn't bow down now, Kobayakawa would be sure to get at Sagami. That was the only thing that stopped Tatsurou from resisting.

Damn it!

He was angry, but had no choice. This was his only option now. He would only lose his pride, after all, nothing really important.

"F-fine," Tatsurou spat out.

Kobayakawa ordered his henchmen to release the captive.

Tatsurou put his hands on the floor and bowed. Inside, he boiled over with anger and humiliation, but he lowered his face to the ground as humbly as he could.

"I'm sorry. Please forgive me," he mumbled, his voice trembling with rage.

Kobayakawa kicked Tatsurou's head even lower. "Too high. Get closer to the ground. Give me a real apology."

Tatsurou lowered himself further, his face so close he could kiss the floor.

"I beg you to forgive me. I have behaved badly," he groveled. *I'm doing this for Lovely and Sagami,* he reminded himself.

"Good. Look up now." Kobayakawa lifted his foot from Tatsurou's head.

Tatsurou looked up to see Kobayakawa smirking at him. He seemed to be getting some perverted pleasure out of Tatsurou's humiliation.

But Tatsurou's ordeal wasn't over yet. Now Kobayakawa rifled through Tatsurou's pockets and pulled out a wallet. He removed all the 10,000 bills, then glanced at the gorgeous watch on Tatsurou's wrist.

"Doing well for yourself, aren't you? Where did this come from, the president-to-be?" Kobayakawa asked, his eyes dancing. Then he reached over and grabbed the Rolex, too.

Bastard!

Tatsurou couldn't bear to lose the watch, his first big gift from Sagami. He reached out to get it back, then quickly stopped himself.

But Kobayakawa still noticed, and started to tease him. "You never used to make faces like that! I cried for joy when the Kantou Hinodegumi kicked you out. Wanna know why? Because I hoped then you'd work for us. How about it? Give up that brown-nosing day job and work here. It'll be good for you. We have lots of dangerous stuff to do, more suitable for a guy like you."

Kobayakawa wasn't being kind. All he wanted was a disposable foot soldier. Tatsurou knew that Kobayakawa would use him only for his dirty work. If anything went wrong, Kobayakawa would deny everything, thus saving the Seishoukai's reputation.

"Unfortunately for you, I have cut my ties with the Yakuza world," Tatsurou gritted out.

"Like that's possible," Kobayakawa chortled. But his smile disappeared in the next instant. He glared at Tatsurou like he was boring a hole right through him. "Sorry to hear that. But Yakuza never give up the lifestyle that easily. Now that I know where you work, maybe we can do business together."

His words chilled Tatsurou.

So this won't be the end of it.

That's what Kobayakawa really meant. Now that he knew how Lovely operated, he wouldn't be satisfied with Tatsurou's simple apology. Tatsurou quickly realized just how naïve he had been, and this was only the beginning.

Kobayakawa took a card and slipped it into his pocket, then threw the cardholder back at Tatsurou.

"Do you wanna join me, or do you wanna be foolish?" he asked. "You have until tomorrow to decide."

This sucks.

Tatsurou let out a deep sigh as he headed back to Sagami's apartment.

Kobayakawa would not let things go now, Tatsurou knew that. The best thing now was to distance himself from Sagami.

But I've just gotten used to being with him…

For the first time in his life, Tatsurou felt almost happy with someone. He wanted to stay with Sagami, but he knew he had to leave. He didn't plan to share the gory details with Sagami. That way, if the Seishoukai chased after him, Sagami could be completely oblivious.

I didn't help things. I made them worse.

He looked down at himself with dismay. The beautiful British suit was now stained with coffee. His coat was smudged with footprints and ripped down the back, probably sliced with a knife during the brawl.

Damn it!

He didn't want Sagami to see him looking like this. He paused at the marble pillar outside the building and took a deep breath.

Fuck it.

Sagami could definitely be annoying, but he didn't care about Tatsurou's Yakuza past. No matter how much Tatsurou threatened him, Sagami had never looked the least bit intimidated. The man was either incredibly impressive—or incredibly foolish.

When Sagami had forced them to be a couple, Tatsurou had finally opened up to him. Sagami pampered him and let him be himself.

But I can't be with Sagami anymore.

His heart grew heavy with what he was about to do. His chest tightened, almost like someone was pushing down on it. He had never felt pain like this before. How could he go through with this? His eyes filled with tears, which he couldn't hold back.

Huh?

Was this really him?

Tatsurou liked being with Sagami, that was certain. Nothing more, nothing less. But why was he feeling so much pain? He felt utterly lost. Biting down on his lip, he sobbed like a little girl.

What the hell's wrong with me?

He couldn't believe himself. The former boss of the Hinodegumi, who once struck fear in the hearts of men, was bawling like a baby? What the hell had Sagami done to him? He scowled, rubbed his eyes, and looked up at the sky.

Sagami.

Just thinking about him made Tatsurou feel warm inside. He wanted Sagami to hold him tight. He wanted Sagami to tell him everything would be all right.

This was what he had always wanted, always needed. He liked Sagami way more than he ever thought he would. But only now, when he was about to leave him, could Tatsurou even admit that to himself.

He rubbed his eyes again with his fists, then thrust them into his pockets. He looked over the payment demand for Heart System.

He had hoped to collect the money and then gallantly present it to Sagami. He wanted to prove he was useful to him, despite the opinions of those high and mighty executives.

But that just wouldn't be possible now.

He wanted to just put the payment demand in Sagami's mailbox and leave without saying goodbye, though he desperately wanted to see him. He knew this might be their last chance together. His chest tightened again. He felt so much for Sagami, he knew that now. And though he also knew that leaving without saying goodbye would be easier for both of them, he still couldn't bring himself to do it.

He checked his reflection in the hallway, making sure he looked calm, then headed for Sagami's apartment.

Sagami smiled and opened the door for Tatsurou

as soon as he heard his voice on the intercom. Usually, he asked Tatsurou to come over. This was the first time Tatsurou had come on his own, so Sagami was more than a little surprised to see him.

"C'mon in," he said. "What's wrong? Did something happen?"

Tatsurou took one look at Sagami and turned as white as a ghost. He kept his eyes on Sagami as he stepped inside. He originally planned to just hand over the payment demand and leave, but his body had other ideas.

Sagami looked good even just hanging out at home, wearing a soft shirt over casual pants. He always managed to look like he was living the high life. The apartment felt cozy and warm, as did the soft, fluffy carpet. Tatsurou would have loved to sit and relax for a while, but that was definitely out of the question.

"What's wrong? You look all beat up," Sagami commented.

"I, uh, had a little trouble," Tatsurou replied.

"You were in a fight?" Sagami asked. "Your coat's a real mess."

Tatsurou had worried that Sagami would scold him for ruining the expensive suit, but Sagami's tone was gentle. There was not even a hint of anger, only concern. Tatsurou felt so guilty and pathetic. All of Sagami's concern was just wasted on a thug like him.

"Well, it didn't suit me, did it?" he retorted, tossing the coat on the floor. The truth was he'd absolutely loved that coat and the fancy suit. But he had to show Sagami he was different from him.

It has to end here.

His brain felt foggy. Maybe he should start an argument. That would be easier for both of them. Sagami would never come looking for him then. And if Kobayakawa came around, Sagami could truthfully say he knew nothing of Tatsurou's whereabouts. Right now, Tatsurou needed to make Sagami hate his guts.

He yanked off the tie and threw it on top of the coat, then took off the suit, grabbed the payment demand, and handed it to Sagami.

"I couldn't collect this," he growled.

"Really?" Sagami asked, surprised. "Even you couldn't get the money back? That's a real problem."

"Heart System is in trouble," Tatsurou explained gruffly. "The Seishoukai sold all the real estate. Our only option is to bargain with them for a share."

Maybe Sagami can give the job to someone else. They could negotiate and recover at least some of the debt. Tatsurou didn't mention their threats, however.

"The Yakuza don't give up money that easily. To deal with Yakuza, I should use other Yakuza," Sagami considered. "Should I hire another gang? Either way it'll cost a ton of money. Collection might well be impossible."

He sighed and put the payment demand on the table, then reached out and grabbed Tatsurou's hand.

Tatsurou looked at him with surprise, then hung his head in shame. He just couldn't make eye contact right now.

"Did you wind up like this because of the money?" Sagami asked cautiously.

"Of course not," Tatsurou lied quickly. "That had nothing to do with this. I bumped into an old acquaintance, that's all."

"An old acquaintance?" Sagami prompted, sharp as ever.

Tatsurou had to be careful or he'd wind up spilling the beans. He'd better leave as soon as possible. He got up from the sofa.

"Where's my old suit?" he demanded. "That white one I used to wear?"

"I had it dry-cleaned," Sagami said, taking the suit out of a closet and handing it to Tatsurou.

"What happened to your watch?" he asked as Tatsurou took off his shirt.

He must have grabbed my hand to check for the Rolex.

Rendered almost speechless by Sagami's sharpness, Tatsurou snorted. "Oh, that. I sold it. Creeped me out, having matching watches."

"You needed the money?" Sagami probed.

"Sure," Tatsurou said. "I always do. I mean, I owe you money. I'm sick of being buried in debt with a guy like you."

He was really trying his best to make Sagami despise him. He removed the gold business card holder from his suit pocket and pressed it against Sagami's chest.

Kobayakawa had his card now. If something happened, Kobayakawa could use it as evidence of Tatsurou's connection to Lovely. No matter how much Tatsurou claimed otherwise, the card imprinted with

Lovely's logo proved he worked for them. If the police investigated, it would be Exhibit A.

"You've been good to me, but I need to disappear for a while," Tatsurou said in a rush, trying to end it quickly.

Sagami looked shocked. He grabbed Tatsurou's hand and pushed him against the wall. "What happened? Please tell me."

Tatsurou knew Sagami was really upset, but he just glared back at him.

Sagami's usual self-confidence was swiftly deserting him. Tatsurou felt both elated and sorrowful at having this power over Sagami. For a moment, they said nothing, just kept looking at each other.

Tatsurou knew they were feeling the same emotions, but he managed not to shed a tear. He had deceived people so easily as a Yakuza, jumping right into a life of crime while leaving his morals behind. Why did lying to Sagami now hurt so badly?

He decided to be as heartless as possible. He needed to make his words drip with poison.

"I'm bored. Can't breathe around you. Let me do what I want for a while," he said bluntly.

"Bored?" Sagami whispered.

Now he looked hurt. Tatsurou's words were obviously tearing him apart.

I have to do it. I have to protect Sagami.

Tatsurou had expected Sagami to wildly protest. That's what should have happened, but Sagami totally surprised him.

"You still have to pay the debt back,"

Sagami said firmly.

Tatsurou bellowed in rage, channeling all the pain of knowing that Sagami only cared about his money.

"I'd love to tell you to fuck off," he yelled. "But if you want it, take it now. Whatever you wanna do to me, do it. You just want my body, right? Well here it is! Take what I owe you."

He knew he didn't really mean it, but he had to do this for Sagami's sake.

"Just your body," Sagami said in a sarcastic tone.

He grabbed Tatsurou's chin, forcing him to look up. It wasn't like Sagami to be this angry.

This needed to happen.

Tatsurou had pushed Sagami around before, but he had never gone this far. But even Sagami's patience had its limits. He roughly squeezed Tatsurou's jaw again, making Tatsurou bite his tongue.

"You wanna hear something?" Tatsurou sneered.

"What?"

Tatsurou's heart skipped a beat, but he narrowed his eyes and smiled, trying to provoke Sagami even more.

"I'm sick of you," he hissed. "I've had enough of your sick hobby."

He threw off Sagami's hand and tried to push him away. Sagami slammed him back against the wall.

"Then you better pay me back," Sagami demanded, his eyes cold and piercing.

His eyes weren't laughing anymore.

Now Tatsurou was on his knees, his mouth around another man's penis. Never had he stooped so low.

He never imagined it would come to this. Though he could hardly believe it himself, this was definitely happening.

His mouth was wide open, lips tightly sealed around Sagami's cock. The only way he could breathe was through his nose. As he ran his tongue over Sagami's member, Sagami held his hair away from his face. Tatsurou felt awkward, having never done this before, but Sagami really seemed to be enjoying it.

He's watching me...

Tatsurou felt Sagami's eyes boring into him. A drop of saliva escaped his mouth and dripped down his chin.

No matter how many times he'd been with Sagami, Tatsurou still felt very embarrassed and shy. Having Sagami's big cock in his mouth made the blood rush right to his head. His own desires flared up, even though his body remained untouched. Each time he licked Sagami, he felt the heat inside him starting to rise.

"Nice job, Tatsurou," Sagami said breathlessly.

Tatsurou frowned, but continued. Sagami was getting bigger and harder with each lick. Tatsurou could no longer get it all in his mouth. It was getting hard to breathe.

How long can I keep this up? Tatsurou wondered, starting to feel impatient. His mouth made a weird sucking sound as he jerked his head up and down.

"Never thought I could get you to do this," Sagami sighed, his voice dripping with desire.

Why am I doing this? I'm supposed to be breaking up with him.

Tatsurou opened his eyes to see Sagami looking down at him. He knew his eyes were watering and his ears were red. He kept sucking on Sagami's penis and groaned.

He was quickly losing control. He had intended to lie his way out of having sex today, but it was getting harder and harder to conceal his lust.

His body knew he wanted Sagami. His body *never* lied.

Sagami squinted at him.

"Looks like you enjoy it," he mocked. "Your legs are shaking. Try fingering yourself. Push your finger deep inside and pleasure yourself. If you do, I'll fuck you later."

Sagami's suggestion sent Tatsurou's head spinning, but Tatsurou did as told, like some perverted puppet. With Sagami still in his mouth, he loosened his belt, unzipped his pants, and pulled them down. He was already rock hard.

"Don't touch your cock," Sagami ordered, sounding forceful. His harsh tone made Tatsurou tremble a little.

Tatsurou wanted to touch himself so badly.

Caress his warm, erect penis. Jerk himself off. He knew it would feel great right now, but he also knew that following Sagami's orders was part of the excitement. He spread his legs a little. Making sure he didn't touch his penis, his hand darted between his buttocks.

He gently massaged the outside first, but soon realized his fingers were too dry. He took his mouth away from Sagami's penis and sucked on his own finger.

"Such a dirty boy," Sagami teased.

Tatsurou looked up at him. Sagami's gaze was so penetrating, Tatsurou's eyes filled with tears. Then he put his moistened finger in the hole between his buttocks.

"Agh…"

As soon as his fingers touched the spot, his body shivered in anticipation. From his mouth came a muffled groan as he slowly pushed his finger inside the warm passage. His muscles clamped around his finger, caressing it. He pushed his mouth down even further on Sagami's penis.

"I think you like sucking my cock," Sagami continued to tease. "But I'll stop you right before I come. I want to come on your face."

My face?!

Tatsurou's body seemed to understand quicker than his mind did, since his heart instantly started to race. Just the thought of it made him almost come.

Feeling agitated and a little confused, he kept fingering himself, desperately hoping for release. He still felt tight inside, but was getting looser with each thrust of his finger. He felt so embarrassed to be seen like this that his legs quivered.

"Ngh…ngh…ngh…"

Sagami tenderly stroked his hair, holding his head so it wouldn't shake. Tatsurou's breathing became even more erratic. His mouth was full of Sagami's cock. Sagami was staring down at him so intensely. Tatsurou felt the weight of the gaze almost physically. The movement of his mouth and the contractions in his anus seemed linked by a strange rhythm. Now his finger was completely inside, but it wasn't enough to relieve his desperation.

Suddenly, Sagami reached under Tatsurou's shirt and pulled on his nipples, which already stood at attention. As Sagami tweaked them between his fingers, Tatsurou contracted hard on the finger inside him. His spine tingled, and he trembled even more than before, helplessly searching for relief.

With Sagami's cock deep in his throat, he gasped for breath.

"If you're going to come, do it so I can watch," Sagami ordered.

Tatsurou trembled again. This could actually make him come? True, his body was reaching its limits. Sagami's fingers, his own finger, and his mouth all moved in unison. Something was building up inside, a wave of pure bliss washing right over him.

"Ng…ah, ah, ah…"

His mouth moved faster and faster on Sagami's penis. Sagami pushed his cock deeper into Tatsurou's mouth. Tatsurou gasped for breath as his tongue, his nipples, and his G-spot all helped him find ecstasy.

Tatsurou sped up, about to reach his climax. Sagami suddenly let go of his nipples and groaned. The penis inside Tatsurou's mouth pulsed and swelled. Tatsurou felt a warm drop of liquid on his tongue from the tip of Sagami's cock.

"Ngh…!"

All of a sudden, Tatsurou moved his mouth away and turned his head, but he was a second too late. Warm semen spurted over his face, running down his cheeks, his nose, his lips.

Tatsurou had never felt so perverted—or so happy.

"Now you look really good," Sagami panted.

Tatsurou was still gasping for breath as his body burned. His heart was beating so fast he was afraid it would break. *Sagami can't see me like this!*

"Shut up!" he yelled.

But Sagami just pushed him to the floor. He pinned down Tatsurou's arms with his knees and then opened his legs wide. Then Sagami pushed his fingers inside Tatsurou's already burning body.

"Looks like you're ready for me," Sagami mused.

Tatsurou quivered as Sagami fingered him, tossing his head from side to side. He was so close to coming. All he wanted now was Sagami thrusting inside him. His whole body cried out for it. He pushed his ass against Sagami's hand, trying to feel him more deeply, his body now acting on its own. He had completely lost any self-control.

"Bit of a pervert now, aren't we?" Sagami

snorted. "My fingers aren't enough, you want something thicker inside. Will you find someone else to do this when I'm not around?"

"Ngh! Ah! Ah!"

Tatsurou felt consumed with pleasure as he moved in rhythm, wanting it harder and harder.

The tip of Sagami's cock was so close to his ass now. That alone was enough to get his juices flowing.

Sagami mounted him, his hard penis penetrating deep inside Tatsurou. It went all the way in, hitting Tatsurou's G-spot.

"Ah…" Tatsurou could only groan now. A violent pleasure was spreading from his ass to the rest of his body.

I'm going to come…

His vision filled with a bright light, his entire body focused on his impending orgasm. Just then, Sagami squeezed the base of Tatsurou's penis, stopping his orgasm in its tracks.

"Ngh…ah, ah, ah…"

Lost in a wave of pleasure that never peaked, Tatsurou groaned with agony. His body felt so numb, he thought he would faint. He gripped Sagami's penis tightly, enjoying the warmth and the hardness. There was an intense, overwhelming bliss mixed in with the frustration of not ejaculating.

"Ngh…ah, Ah…wha…"

"You can't come yet, Tatsurou," Sagami hissed. "I want to teach you about real pain."

Tatsurou just glowered at Sagami, unable to reply. Sagami's cock was still deep inside him. Each breath Tatsurou took sent stabbing pain throughout his body.

Why is he doing this?

His whole body had been ready to come since he started sucking Sagami's penis. He couldn't stay still and didn't think even more pleasure was possible.

Just then, Sagami violently thrust into Tatsurou, whose sensitive body had no resistance left. Tatsurou moaned over and over again. Trying to calm the pain, he draped his arm over Sagami's shoulder.

"Ngh, mmmmm, ah…"

Tatsurou felt weak, all of his power gone. His mouth hung wide open, dripping saliva from each corner. The sounds of Sagami's thrusts and Tatsurou's moans reverberated around the room, yet Tatsurou still didn't come.

"Mmmm…ah, ah, ah…"

Tatsurou gritted his teeth as Sagami kept thrusting. His muscles contracted over and over again, an overwhelming pleasure that was impossible to ignore. His aching desire for gratification now totally consumed him.

"Ready to come?" Sagami whispered sweetly.

Tatsurou could only nod. He just wanted to shoot off as fast as possible, giddy from the feeling of being penetrated. Every sensation he felt was building to his orgasm.

"Ah, right. Better take a rest then," Sagami said suddenly, holding back his thrusts.

Everything stopped. Tatsurou's legs twitched. He needed to finish, now! His eyes watered as he let out a noise that sounded like a sob.

"No…please…" he begged.

He wanted it so much, his hips shuddered. He propped himself up on his elbows, lifted his crotch, and pushed back on Sagami's member with all his might.

Sagami smiled and let go of Tatsurou's penis. "Go ahead. Try moving a little faster."

"Ah, ah, ngh…"

Tatsurou raised and lowered his hips, pushing Sagami's cock in deeper each time. He definitely felt something, but not nearly enough to reach a climax. Finally, he stopped in frustration.

"Quitting already? Maybe I should just take it out," Sagami said, starting to move away.

Tatsurou instantly pushed him back in again.

"DON'T TAKE IT OUT! I'LL MOVE!" he gasped. He desperately moved back and forth again, panting like a dog. "Ah, ah…Ngh, mmmm…"

Each time he moved, he saw Sagami inside him, but he didn't even care. He just kept moving up and down, in and out. When Sagami's penis hit a spot that felt especially good, he positioned his hips to make sure he'd hit it again and again.

"Ah…ah…"

Tears streamed down his face, and he barely knew what he was doing anymore. Suddenly Sagami grabbed his hips and thrust even deeper into him.

"AH!"

That almost made him come. His body shuddered again as he felt a tingle down his spine. Sagami's penis was closer and closer to bringing the ejaculation he so desperately desired.

But then, Sagami stopped again.

"Why?" Tatsurou whined.

He was in sheer agony now. His orgasm felt so close, only to be snatched away. He was more frantic than ever.

"I'm teaching you something. Showing you pleasure, so you never ever leave me," Sagami explained.

"No...I..." Tatsurou stammered.

The pain he could stand, but this pleasure was unbearable. Sagami thrust in again, keeping Tatsurou in the peak of pleasure. But it felt like torture to Tatsurou now.

"I wonder how much you can take," Sagami said.

He stroked Tatsurou's stiff penis, then grabbed the base and squeezed hard. Tatsurou groaned again.

Sagami wasn't pleasuring Tatsurou, he was tormenting him. As Sagami started thrusting again, Tatsurou knew Sagami would never let him come.

"No...please...no more..."

Tatsurou had had more than enough of this cruel excitement. Each thrust exploded like a rocket inside him. He tensed his stomach muscles and tried to hold back, but just felt Sagami even more.

"Ngh, ah...ah...ah..."

"You're really tight now. Enjoying it?" Sagami taunted.

As Tatsurou desperately tried to escape this tortuous pleasure, he started to get angry.

Enough was enough, and now he was sobbing like a baby.

"Sagami please! I beg you!" he pleaded.

"Then tell me now," Sagami growled. "Tell me why you're leaving me."

"No…reason…ah, ah, AH!" Tatsurou gasped, struggling to stop his tears.

Frustrated, he started groping his own chest. He grabbed his tight, swollen nipples. Touching them just made it worse, but he couldn't stop himself. He had had way too much now, and felt numb all over.

He gasped like a crazed animal as Sagami started thrusting again.

Sagami pushed Tatsurou's pleasure to the final peak, but the orgasm never came. The pleasure was only in his mind, but his body still convulsed.

"AH…!"

He felt Sagami come inside him. Sagami kissed and consoled him, then started to move again. He would give Tatsurou absolutely no mercy.

"No…no…more…" Tatsurou panted.

"I won't stop," Sagami answered. "Not until I get some answers."

This was Tatsurou's sexual purgatory.

The ringing phone interrupted Sagami's sleep.

He opened his eyes a crack and let out a little sigh. Tatsurou had taken off. After abusing him until the breaking point, Sagami had carried the unconscious Tatsurou to bed. The man should have been right next to him, soundly asleep.

Sagami touched the pillow. Stone cold. Tatsurou must have left some time ago.

Where did he go?

Tatsurou couldn't have had much sleep. Hell, he probably couldn't even walk. But he still managed to leave somehow. He really didn't want to be with Sagami.

Sagami sighed, feeling his heart sink into a gloomy abyss. He didn't want to talk to anybody, but the phone kept ringing, demanding his attention.

He picked it up, resigned to his fate. The instant he put it to his ear, he heard Hachi's anguished voice.

"Is he...is he there?" Hachi gasped.

"No," Sagami answered dully. "He didn't come back home?"

Holding the cordless receiver, Sagami got out of the bed and opened the shades. The sun was already up. He had slept longer than usual. If he didn't get moving, he'd be late for his nine o'clock meeting.

Does it really matter?

He felt as if all the energy had been sapped out of him. His relationship with Tatsurou had been going so well. Now, in just one night, it was all over.

What did I do wrong?

Maybe Tatsurou was actually straight as an arrow after all. Being with a man had become too much for him.

"It's terrible!" Hachi exclaimed. "People say he's been kidnapped by a gang!"

Sagami immediately came to his senses.

"Kidnapped?" he echoed.

"I just heard about it now," Hachi babbled. "It happened early this morning. Boss was walking downtown, drunk out of his mind. Some thugs jumped him and threw him in a car. Then I got a phone call, someone from the Seishoukai, I think. The Seishoukai members are old enemies of the boss, especially Kobayakawa, their Tokyo branch president. If Kobayakawa took him, the boss is dead meat!"

Sagami had heard of Kobayakawa before. The man was quite a powerful figure. Hachi probably wasn't exaggerating this time, though like most Yakuza Hachi loved to exaggerate. Even now, the thought made Sagami smile a little.

Tatsurou in trouble with Kobayakawa?

Sagami wondered if he should even get involved. The Yakuza world had its own, violent customs. But Tatsurou hadn't gone with them willingly, he'd been kidnapped. He was plagued with doubts.

As Hachi babbled on anxiously, Sagami interrupted him. "Maybe Tatsurou knew them. Maybe Tatsurou is returning to his old life."

He felt a sharp pain in his chest as he remembered last night. He had asked Tatsurou why he was leaving, over and over again, but Tatsurou only said he was bored.

"That can't be!" Hachi insisted. "The boss loved his new life. He used to get drunk and tell me how happy he was now. He loved the suit you gave him so much, he wouldn't even let me touch it. He gave me one of the business cards, too. No way would he ever join the gang again. The boss may be proud, but he's also loyal."

Hachi hit the nail right on the head.

Sagami suddenly felt he understood everything.

Tatsurou had definitely acted weird last night. He wouldn't even look at him. And Sagami could tell he was feeling unsure of himself. Even after Sagami had asked for the payment once a month, Tatsurou had still acted strange.

"Did Tatsurou actually tell you he was going straight?" he asked Hachi.

But his mind was already made up. So what if Tatsurou had broken up with him? If Tatsurou had been kidnapped, then he had to do something. He would get rid of anything that prevented Tatsurou from living an honest, decent life.

Energy swelled up inside him.

"Understood," he said firmly. "I'll look into it. Where was Tatsurou kidnapped?"

After Hachi explained, Sagami immediately hung up. He knew the location well. In fact, the act might have even been caught on camera. He made a few phone calls to have that looked into, then let Lovely know he was taking the day off. He could easily make up for the time. Right now, Tatsurou was his top priority.

I don't care about overstepping the bounds. I don't care if he still wants to break up. He needs my help.

It hurt like hell to be rejected by someone you loved. Maybe Sagami was only picking at his wound, but he wouldn't give up on Tatsurou.

He had first seen Tatsurou way back in high

school. Tatsurou was his first love, in fact. His only love, Sagami knew in his heart.

What spurred him on the most was the chance of seeing Tatsurou again. It wouldn't be easy to find him, but Sagami would use his whole organization if necessary. Just the thought of Tatsurou made Sagami's eyes start to shine again.

Tatsurou woke up with a stinking hangover.
Where am I? Why am I here?

He was in a dreary room, surrounded by concrete walls. The only furniture was a shabby bed, a battered desk, and a metal chair. He was sprawled on the bed, covered by a thin blanket.

He stared at the ceiling with half-open eyes. He really could use a cigarette.
Damn. I'm all out.

After staggering out of Sagami's house the night before, he had gone drinking. He was totally plastered when Kobayakawa found him.
That bastard! Threatening me!

"I had to take my employees that *you* punched to see a doctor," Kobayakawa had said. "I also had to file a report. Now everyone will know who beat them up. It was Tatsurou Yamamoto, Lovely Kantou Branch, Assistant to the Branch Manager. If I went to the police now, there'd be a big scandal. Wouldn't look good for your boss, either."

If he didn't want to cause trouble for Sagami, Tatsurou had no choice but to work for Kobayakawa.

But he knew Kobayakawa would only use him and toss him away. If he did the Seishoukai's dirty work, it was only a matter of time before he was picked up for something. But at least his deal with Kobayakawa would let Sagami off the hook.

Tatsurou had climbed into Kobayakawa's car to talk it over with him, despite the fact he felt totally wasted. The smooth motion of the car, along with his exhaustion from being used by Sagami, had put Tatsurou right to sleep.

Oh. I must be in Shinjuku. This must be the Seishoukai office.

He sat up, but lacked the energy to look out the window. He sighed and smelled his breath, which reeked of alcohol. He rubbed his temples, wishing that he had some Tylenol. His head was now pounding.

Then the metal door burst open. In came Kobayakawa, wearing a fine suit. Three minions pompously followed behind him.

"You're up already? Still drunk?" Kobayakawa scoffed.

"I'm not drunk," Tatsurou said.

He swung his legs off the bed as Kobayakawa's henchmen eyed him with hostility. They looked more than ready to start a fight. One had a bruised face. Tatsurou vaguely remembered punching the guy.

He looked casually around the room, searching for a possible weapon. He really needed a metal pipe, but there was only the metal chair. If it came down to it, he'd have to fight with his fists.

"You probably don't remember how you got

here," Kobayakawa said. "One of my men had to prop you on the bed or you would have fallen asleep on the floor."

"Cut the crap," Tatsurou growled.

"Don't speak to me like that. You have to follow every single order that I give. Remember that," Kobayakawa sneered, looking crazed.

Tatsurou turned his head and cursed to himself. But he had to keep quiet, even when the boss insulted him. The other men still looked angry.

"Sir, let us teach him a lesson," one suggested.

Tatsurou scoffed. He was in no mood to be intimidated by lowlifes. Besides, the way that Kobayakawa was gawking at him really bothered him. He returned the look with an arrogant stare, while Kobayakawa talked to his men.

"Wait," Kobayakawa ordered then turned back to Tatsurou. "First let's see how useful you are. You already bowed to me. This time, kiss my shoe and beg like a dog to join the Seishoukai."

Kobayakawa looked euphoric. He pulled out the business card and flashed it at Tatsurou. Seeing it again made Tatsurou boil with rage. Because of this bastard, he'd had to leave Sagami and step back into the murky Yakuza world.

If he could get the business card back, there would be no physical evidence he was ever affiliated with Lovely. He had to make that a priority.

He was livid beyond words, surrounded by Yakuza in the enemy camp. No matter how strong he was, he could never overpower them all. Still, he didn't intend to kiss and make up yet.

He slowly stood up and looked at Kobayakawa. Everyone in the room felt the tension and froze, waiting to see what would happen next.

Tatsurou moved closer to Kobayakawa. The Yakuza's henchmen scurried to protect him.

"I told you to kiss my shoe!" Kobayakawa ordered.

Tatsurou pushed some men aside and kneeled down. Then he lowered his head, waiting for just the right moment.

In a flash, he grabbed the card from Kobayakawa's hand.

"Bastard!" Kobayakawa cried out.

The men moved faster than Kobayakawa and tried to grab Tatsurou's shoulders.

Throwing them off, Tatsurou swung his fist up.

"Get the fuck off!" he yelled.

First there was a cracking sound, then a man fell back, blood dripping from his nose.

The other henchmen went berserk cursing Tatsurou.

"BASTARD!"

"Get him!"

Tatsurou dashed to the window and quickly opened it. It was blocked by metal bars, making escape impossible. He slipped the business card through a crack and out into the world. The wind instantly picked it up and blew it away.

Suddenly, he sensed someone behind him. He ducked just as a fist skimmed his head.

Now he was trapped in an all-out fight, as even bigger thugs arrived to help their comrades.

Tatsurou staggered, completely out of breath. Even his strong body had its limits. Besides, his opponents weren't ordinary men, they were Yakuza.

"Ngh," he grunted.

Sweat dripped down his forehead, clouding his vision and stinging his eyes. He blinked to try and clear them and got punched. Someone pinned his arms behind his back, while another thug punched his gut over and over again, without mercy.

"Ngh. Ah…" He puked onto the floor, then gasped for breath.

"Stop there," Kobayakawa's voice rang out. He wasn't trying to save Tatsurou, he just wanted to torture him more slowly.

Emerging from the shadows, Kobayakawa looked at Tatsurou, whose chest heaved as his lungs gulped in air. Kobayakawa yanked up Tatsurou by his hair.

"I won't let you fall unconscious," he hissed. "Now we get serious."

Serious?!

Tatsurou looked at Kobayakawa and tried to spit, but his mouth was far too dry. That last hit had knocked the wind out of him.

Kobayakawa leaned closer. "I've waited to see you cry for so long. I want to see you really sob, so I'll let every man here have a go at you."

"What the…?" Tatsurou cried out.

He didn't understand what Kobayakawa was saying. Did something happen between them that he should know about? Unfortunately, he couldn't really think straight right now. His bones ached too much from having his arms pinned back for so long.

Kobayakawa pulled out a knife and placed it against Tatsurou's chest. Tatsurou saw his reflection in the blade and gulped. Then Kobayakawa playfully moved the knife down the front of Tatsurou's jacket, popping the buttons off one by one before ripping the crimson shirt underneath.

"What is it?" Tatsurou croaked.

Now Kobayakawa caressed Tatsurou's smooth skin with the blade, teasing him. He didn't cut the skin, but the cold metal made Tatsurou shiver and his hair stand on end.

The marks from last night were still there. He didn't come last night, but his body felt different than normal.

As the knife's tip grazed his nipple, Tatsurou shuddered.

"Ngh."

His tiny, reflexive movement pushed the knife into his white skin. A trickle of blood oozed down his chest.

It was only a graze, but his bloodstained nipple changed the mood in the room into something much wilder. He could hear people swallowing hard, as the mood became even darker.

He bit his lip and glared at Kobayakawa. This

only seemed to excite the men more.

Sagami parked his Lincoln Navigator in front of the Seishoukai office.

Usually someone would come out to meet him, but no one did today. Hachi nervously glanced at Sagami. It was obvious that something was up.

One of Sagami's contacts had given him the surveillance video from the location where Tatsurou had been kidnapped. Sagami had watched the footage just a little while ago.

Spotting Tatsurou in the film was easy. He stood out in his pure-white suit. Sagami watched as the drunk Tatsurou was forced into a gangster's car. Hachi was sure the man who had taken Tatsurou was Kobayakawa of the Seishoukai.

The Seishoukai had several offices in the city, but Hachi had a hunch they'd taken Tatsurou to Shinjuku. The office was a large building, just outside the downtown area. There were few people around at night, and the building itself looked onto a lonely street filled with trashcans.

Hachi followed Sagami inside. Sagami had already decided that he wouldn't use force, but he heard something going on in a back room.

"I'll make you wish you'd never been born," a voice growled.

"Argh! Oof!"

Those could only be Tatsurou's cries. Sagami felt anxious for his safety, and wanted to find him right away. With all of his strength, Sagami kicked open the thick metal door. To his immense surprise, it crashed to the floor. He figured the hinges must have been loose. He was strong, but not *that* strong.

A man standing behind the door had been thrown down with it and was now rolling around on the floor. Sagami grabbed the man's collar.

"Where is Tatsurou?" he asked gruffly.

He made sure his voice revealed that he would show no mercy to whoever got in his way. The man passed out before he could answer.

"Hachi! Let's go!" Sagami barked, shoving the man aside. They moved toward the back of the building, heading towards all the commotion. All of a sudden, the noise stopped. Sagami knew that if he didn't hurry, something terrible might happen, something that even he couldn't fix.

Sagami fought off nearly 20 Yakuza to get inside that room.

Driven by pure, unadulterated rage, he quickly defeated the Yakuza who jumped him. His skill in martial arts made it easy for him to target an enemy's weak point for a quick take-down. The narrow corridor helped, too, since he faced only one opponent at a time.

He felt the tension in the room as a tangible, physical force. The room was filled with low-life thugs. At their feet, he thought he saw a flash of white.

Tatsurou?

Without a second thought, Sagami pushed the

men out of his way to get a clearer view. It was Tatsurou! The instant he saw him, Sagami tightly clenched his fists, punching anyone who came near him.

"What have you done to him?!" he screamed.

Suddenly, he heard a shallow laugh. A rather intellectual-looking man stood proudly in front of Tatsurou. The man spoke deliberately, choosing his words with care.

"So you're the nobleman. You've got some guts coming in here and starting a fight all on your own. We were just showing Tatsurou a thing or two. He hates following orders, doesn't he? I only cut off his shirt buttons and he threw himself at me."

Shirt buttons?

Sagami understood everything perfectly now. He finally knew what Tatsurou had been trying to do.

"You must be Kobayakawa," he said grimly.

He knew it, even without Hachi's confirmation. Hachi was currently elsewhere, left behind in the wake of Sagami's rampage.

Sagami proceeded to waste each man in the room, one by one. Even though he was just one person, he overwhelmed them like a demon in disguise. His fighting skills were so great, even the Yakuza couldn't touch him. He gradually took over the room, a testament to his superiority over the goons.

"It's over for you now," he grunted as he disposed of the last henchman.

"You bastard!" Kobayakawa shrieked, swinging his fists.

Sagami easily dodged away. Though Kobayakawa

looked intellectual, he had clearly been trained to fight.

Sagami still had the advantage, however. He grabbed Kobayakawa's arm, twisted it, and pushed Kobayakawa to the floor. Now that Kobayakawa was on his knees, Sagami roughly kicked his back.

"What are you doing?!" Hachi screamed, running into the room.

"Hachi?" Kobayakawa whispered.

He suddenly seemed to lose all his desire to fight. Sagami stopped and looked around.

Still in his teens, Hachi's face had the vestiges of youth. He briskly walked toward them, grabbed Kobayakawa by his collar, and slapped him across the face.

Sagami was shocked that Kobayakawa didn't back away. The man could have avoided that slap if he had wanted to.

"Ngh," Kobayakawa grunted.

"I'm disappointed in you, Kobayakawa," Hachi said.

"What?" Kobayakawa mumbled.

Ever since Hachi had arrived, all of Kobayakawa's focus had been on him. Sagami didn't understand what it meant. The pair continued talking.

"What did you do to the boss?!" Hachi screamed. "If you hurt him, I'll never forgive you!"

"Yeah? Well I should never forgive you! I can't believe you moved in with Tatsurou," Kobayakawa squawked. A while ago, he'd been cool as ice. Now he was blushing beet red.

Sagami frowned as he watched this

alarming development.

Hachi snarled at Kobayakawa, who was now groveling before him. "What, jealous? The boss is good-looking, unlike you. A man to admire! You could never even come close to him!"

As Hachi kept spitting out insults, Kobayakawa just listened. Sagami had never witnessed this power in Hachi until now. Bemused, he just watched the scene unfold.

It seemed Hachi and Kobayakawa knew each other from before. Sagami studied Kobayakawa's face as he quietly listened to what Hachi was saying.

Looks like a lover's quarrel, Sagami thought.

"Hachi," Sagami said quietly.

Their conversation seemed like it was going to drag on forever, and Sagami was worried about Tatsurou. Though Tatsurou had no obvious injuries, he was still unconscious. Sagami desperately wanted to pick him up and take him away from this place, but something still had to be done about Kobayakawa.

"Do you know him?" he asked Hachi.

"Nope" was the immediate reply.

"Don't give me that, Hachi," Kobayakawa whined. "We used to hang out together. You used to be fond of me."

"Hmph, pervert," Hachi snapped.

"When you told me you wanted to be a Yakuza, I told you to go for it, remember?" Kobayakawa griped. "Come back to me when you've become a great man, I said. Then I find out you've been working for Tatsurou…"

"If you've done anything to the boss, I'll kill

you, Kobayakawa!" Hachi yelled.

Apparently, Hachi had not returned Kobayakawa's affections. From an outsider's point of view, Kobayakawa was a pitiful sight, but considering what he did to Tatsurou, Sagami had absolutely zero sympathy for him.

"Kobayakawa, what did you do to Tatsurou?" Sagami asked.

Kobayakawa had clearly lost all will to fight. Sagami pushed him out of the way and went over to Tatsurou. As he cradled Tatsurou's limp body, Sagami lightly tapped his cheek. There was no reaction.

"Kobayakawa, there's more to this story, isn't there?" Sagami asked calmly, but with a hint of his growing rage.

Kobayakawa just sighed, severely depressed from his quarrel with Hachi. Since all of his henchmen were out cold, he decided to just give in to Sagami and Hachi.

"Tatsurou came here about that loan from Heart System," he said. "He started the fight first and put two of my men in the hospital. I told him I'd tell the papers that Lovely hires gangsters to do their work. Then Tatsurou bowed and apologized to me."

Bowed?

Sagami's muscles tensed. So that was why Tatsurou had behaved the way he did. That must have been yesterday when Tatsurou had come to his apartment in that filthy suit. His watch was gone, too. But every time Sagami asked what happened, Tatsurou had refused to answer.

"So you threatened him?" Sagami asked.

Kobayakawa gave him a wry smile. Sagami gently put Tatsurou down, then grabbed Kobayakawa's neck.

He was about to slam him to the wall when Hachi screamed, "STOP!"

Though Hachi was infuriated with Kobayakawa, he didn't really hate him. Sagami stopped in his tracks as Hachi turned to face them, looking uncomfortable.

"We don't have to hit him," Hachi said. "He'll talk, won't you?"

Kobayakawa looked intently at Hachi for a moment, then licked his lips and started to talk. Hatred dripped from his every word.

"I told Tatsurou that the hospital knew Lovely's assistant branch manager had beaten up my employees. I also told him we were notifying the police. I said if he didn't want that to happen, then he had to be my man."

"I see now," Sagami muttered.

Kobayakawa had never really threatened Tatsurou. He threatened Lovely, Sagami's family business.

Sagami now knew for sure why Tatsurou had tried to leave him.

You wanted to protect me?

His heart skipped a few beats. Tatsurou had been trying to protect him. He'd taken off and let himself be kidnapped—all for Sagami.

Now that Sagami knew the truth, he had no use for Kobayakawa. He took the payment demand from his pocket and handed it to Hachi.

"Hachi, collect this from Kobayakawa instead

of Tatsurou," he directed.

"Yes. For the boss!" Hachi gladly replied.

"Like hell I'll give you any—" Kobayakawa started to say.

"Just pay up, Kobayakawa," Sagami snapped. "Do you want to make Lovely your enemy? You'll also be paying Tatsurou's medical bills."

Lovely had close ties with the Kantou Asahigumi, plus lots of financial muscle. They'd have absolutely no difficulty finding other regional gangs to hire. All it took was money to have a gang on your side.

Though Kobayakawa didn't seem the type to hush and pay up, he was really tired of fighting. Instead he just nodded.

"Got it," he said tersely.

Out of the corner of his eye, Sagami watched Kobayakawa and Hachi leave, then turned back to Tatsurou.

The front of Tatsurou's suit and shirt had been ripped open, exposing his beautiful bare chest. Sagami noticed a nasty cut near Tatsurou's nipple, but didn't spot any other injuries.

"Tatsurou…" he called gently.

But Tatsurou showed no signs of waking up. His mouth hung slightly open.

Sagami moved a little closer and kissed him.

"Mmmm…" Tatsurou blinked and opened his eyes, but seemed unable to focus on Sagami. His long eyelashes closed again.

Sagami started to panic, fearing that Tatsurou was more seriously injured than he had suspected.

Lifting Tatsurou's long body onto his back, Sagami started to carry him away. He would drive Tatsurou directly to the ER. Then, just as he stepped over the door he had kicked down, Tatsurou made a low sound, hardly a mumble. Sagami could barely make out what he said.

"Think you can...put me in concrete...and feed me to the fishes in Tokyo Bay?" Tatsurou muttered. "That what...you're gonna do? You'll regret it. I have someone...he won't let you...so you better..."

He sounded like he was talking in his sleep. Sagami turned his head to look at Tatsurou's face. He looked so relaxed. *He must be still asleep,* Sagami thought to himself. Maybe he's still confused from the beating he took. Now he thinks they're about to dispose off his body.

When I pulled Tatsurou out of that burning building, he told me his true feelings.

It was the first time Tatsurou had been really honest with Sagami. Would it be the same now? Probably not. Tatsurou was never really disoriented enough to reveal his true feelings, not even when he was drunk. But it was worth a try, anyway.

Trying not to sound too eager, Sagami spoke softly to Tatsurou, taking care not to wake him. "Who is this someone?"

"...You know him," Tatsurou mumbled. "He... he's stronger than me...he has money and power and lots of men. They all call him 'Sir' and 'Mister.' And he...he really loves me. Who knows why...I can be a real jerk...but he'd follow me to hell and back..."

Tatsurou must be talking about him.

He knows I love him.

Hearing Tatsurou say this filled Sagami with joy. He had assumed Tatsurou was still an untamed wildcat. Now it seemed like Tatsurou had finally acknowledged Sagami's deep feelings for him.

"Does he know that this happened to you?" Sagami went on.

He felt so happy now. He wanted to continue this conversation. Tatsurou was bound to wake up soon, and then Sagami would lose this chance to understand him better. Sagami needed to get his answers right now.

"He's sweet…we have a real connection," Tatsurou answered. "Even now, I feel he's with me…I could never leave him…"

We have a real connection?

Did Tatsurou realize, maybe on some subconscious level, that Sagami was carrying him on his back? Sagami felt like hugging him.

"Do you love him back?" he asked cautiously.

Sagami knew that he'd hear the truth this time. Tatsurou had never said he loved him, only that he liked Sagami a lot. But Sagami needed more than that. He held his breath, worrying about the answer.

"Of course…I do."

Sagami's heart jumped for joy. His whole body was listening.

"So do it…kill me," Tatsurou continued. "If you kill me, I'll still find a way to be with Sagami…I love him so much…"

Suddenly, Sagami stopped.

Tatsurou was stirring.

Finally, he had come round. Sagami looked back at him and met Tatsurou's wide-eyed stare.

Huh?

Tatsurou suddenly stiffened all over. He thought he was about to be thrown into Tokyo Bay. He thought he'd been talking to the man who was about to take his life. Was all that just a dream?

No, that wasn't a dream...I definitely said something.

"I love him so much..."

He remembered saying that. He stared blankly into Sagami's eyes. He was on Sagami's back, feeling a soft cashmere coat against his cheek. Under the coat, he felt Sagami's strong, rippling muscles. He must have been so comfortable on Sagami's broad back that he had fallen fast asleep.

But Tatsurou had already broken up with Sagami, vowing never to see him again. Why was Sagami carrying him now? And where the hell was he?

"AH," he suddenly cried out. His head was about to hit a doorframe, but he ducked away in the nick of time.

"Oops...sorry. Are you okay?" Sagami gasped.

Tatsurou saw a metal door lying on the floor. This seemed like the Seishoukai's Shinjuku office, but why was it such a mess? Looked like a car had crashed right into it.

"This is...Seishoukai...," he said. "Why are you...why are you here...?"

"Why?" Sagami echoed. "To get you, of course. I spoke to Kobayakawa, Tatsurou. Now I know why you tried to leave me."

"Where is he?" Tatsurou growled.

"Hachi's getting the money from him," Sagami answered. "Turns out the two of them were childhood friends. In fact, I think Kobayakawa may actually have a thing for Hachi. He was pretty jealous when Hachi came to live with you. I know everything now."

Tatsurou's eyes widened in astonishment.

Everything…everything…everything?

Yes, Sagami seemed to know everything that had happened since Tatsurou had left his apartment. His first reaction was surprise, but that quickly gave way to happiness. Now Tatsurou owed the Seishoukai absolutely nothing. He could be with Sagami again.

"You shouldn't…get in over your head…" he warned, but he was also filled with a strange feeling he didn't quite understand. It was slowly taking him over, like a strong force from inside. He was happy. He never thought being with Sagami would make him so happy. He buried his face into Sagami's back, trying to hide from these new feelings.

Oh…mmm…

It had the opposite effect. Feeling Sagami's warmth and heartbeat made Tatsurou's feelings even more intense. His heart rate sped up as he inhaled deeply, enjoying Sagami's rich smell. It felt so good to be wrapped around him. There was nothing he could do now. For maybe the first time in his life, Tatsurou felt totally satisfied.

I'm like a little girl.

He felt awkward yet fulfilled, and nuzzled his cheek against Sagami's back. Why had Sagami come to a Yakuza office to save him? Such a stupid thing to do, but he wanted to believe it was because Sagami loved him that much.

Sagami has always been an idiot.

Then again, that's what he liked about him. Sagami made Tatsurou feel loved. Right now, Tatsurou was the happiest man in the world.

Sagami exited the building and headed for his nearby Lincoln Navigator. Opening the passenger door, he carefully lowered Tatsurou off his back.

"I'm taking you to the hospital," he declared. "Are you hurt anywhere? How do you feel?"

"I don't need the hospital," Tatsurou replied. "I only lost consciousness from lack of sleep. Some guy was torturing me all night."

"I'm sorry," Sagami said.

Tatsurou lifted his eyes and looked at Sagami. Sagami's face, as usual, was filled with arrogance and confidence. Tatsurou wondered why he was looking like that now, then suddenly remembered.

Did I just tell him I love him?

He had a vague memory of saying something like that. As Sagami's eyes burned into him, Tatsurou turned a bright red color. Even his ears felt hot. But why did he feel so uncomfortable?

"Wha...what are you looking at?" he muttered.

"At least one good thing came out of all this," Sagami said.

"Which was?" Tatsurou prompted.

"I finally discovered how you really feel," Sagami whispered.

As Sagami's beautiful voice filled every part of him, Tatsurou tried to shake off the numbness he felt.

Should I deny it?

He could tell Sagami he didn't mean it. That's what the old Tatsurou would have done.

But...

Sagami had come to his rescue, so just for today, Tatsurou would be nice to him. Actually, he wanted to be intimate with Sagami more than anything. He wanted to feel Sagami's warmth again.

"Come closer," Tatsurou said softly.

He wrapped his arms around Sagami's shoulders, pulling him close. Sagami tightly hugged him back.

"You can hear it again," Tatsurou whispered, "I love you...."

As soon as Tatsurou said it, Sagami pushed him against the headrest, squeezing their lips tightly together.

Sagami must really like him.

The idea no longer seemed so bad to Tatsurou. He had caused Sagami so much trouble, yet Sagami still never abandoned him. Tatsurou now knew Sagami wanted him no matter might happen, no matter what scrapes he managed to get into.

Sagami pried Tatsurou's lips apart with his tongue. As their tongues met and massaged each other, Tatsurou's body filled with excitement. He had had sex with Sagami just that morning, but his body still wasn't satisfied. This time, they would come together properly. His kiss was filled with passion and lust for it.

"Sagami...I want more," he moaned.

He took Sagami's hand and guided it to his exposed skin, but Sagami suddenly pulled away from him. He got into the driver's seat and started the car.

"Let's go somewhere more private," Sagami said.

Tatsurou finally realized they were still outside the Seishoukai office. Not many people were around now, but doing anything more than kissing would be risky.

Sagami drove the Navigator to an underground parking lot a few blocks away. It wasn't pitch black inside, but was only softly illuminated from above.

"No one should see us here," Sagami promised.

He cut the engine and pushed some buttons. Tatsurou's seat slowly reclined until it was almost horizontal.

Whoa.

Tatsurou was now gazing at the roof of the car, his heart pounding. It was the first time he'd ever done it in a car.

Sagami climbed over the seat divider and crawled on top of Tatsurou. He separated Tatsurou's legs, pushing him back on the seat, then started stroking Tatsurou over his clothes.

"What should we do?" Sagami asked.

His hand moved over Tatsurou's crotch from front to back. This alone was enough to excite Tatsurou. Inside their own private space, he heard the sound of his own panting. Being groped over his clothes was more than enough to make him come.

"I...don't...whatever..." he moaned.

He didn't need foreplay. He just wanted Sagami. Now.

Sagami removed Tatsurou's belt and pulled down his pants. Tatsurou still had his shirt on, but most of his chest was exposed from where Kobayakawa had ripped the shirt apart.

"Wanna lick my finger?" Sagami asked, offering one.

Tatsurou rubbed his tongue along it, feeling even more worked up.

Sagami pushed it deeper into Tatsurou's mouth, then took it out. He then placed the same finger on the crevice between Tatsurou's buttocks. The anticipation was enough to get Tatsurou's blood racing.

"You're so...warm," Sagami moaned, pushing his finger inside.

Just like Sagami said, Tatsurou was almost boiling. He already felt on edge, and now a finger was pushed deep inside him. He arched his back at the sensation.

Sagami pushed him back down. "Be careful, you'll hit your head."

Even in a Lincoln Navigator, space was still limited, but that also gave them a good excuse to be even closer than usual.

As Sagami's finger started making little movements, Tatsurou gripped both sides of his seat. Sagami had hit the right spot almost instantly. Tatsurou still felt a little pain, but the intense pleasure easily cancelled that out.

With his other hand, Sagami started to play with Tatsurou's exposed nipples.

"Nn…ah, ah…"

As Sagami kept pinching his nipples, Tatsurou's insides contracted even more. Sagami must have sensed this and pinched even harder.

Tatsurou's body trembled all over. He arched his back and let out a high squeal. "…AH!"

"You dirty boy…do you like this?" Sagami teased, moving his finger more urgently.

Tatsurou's body tensed and he felt his muscles go numb. Sagami knew all of Tatsurou's special places now, and moved his finger even faster.

"Ah…mmmmm…"

Tatsurou felt embarrassed that a small flick of Sagami's finger could turn him into a squirming wreck. But there was nothing he could do anymore.

He was panting loudly, but no one outside could hear them, or so he hoped. Not that it would have mattered to him. He couldn't hold himself back even if people did hear them. He was so close to coming already. His penis was already leaking juice and was hot enough to melt steel. As he started moving his hips again, Sagami whispered to him, "Do you want it? It's a little early but I can."

Tatsurou nodded. Rather, his body nodded for him.

Sagami changed positions. The space that Sagami's finger had left inside immediately closed up. Tatsurou held his breath in anticipation, predicting there would be some pain. Slowly, Sagami pushed. Tatsurou really felt it.

"...Ah!" Tatsurou couldn't take the whole thing at once and cried out a little, instinctively rejecting the foreign object. But this resistance actually increased his desire. Squeezing down on the foreign body made him more turned on. "Ah...ah...ah...wait." He grabbed Sagami's shoulders, gasping for breath. It was still a little painful, so he needed a few seconds to calm down. He needed time to get used to the large member inside him, so large it almost threatened to rip him up.

While still inside Tatsurou, Sagami adjusted himself a little. He slid his body down the seat and lifted Tatsurou on top of him. This pushed him in deeper and made Tatsurou groan. Tatsurou had never been on top before.

Sagami raised his hips.

There was a massive amount of friction. Tatsurou threw his head back and yelped. "AH!"

Apart from being embarrassed at being on top, he was also unsure of what to do.

Sagami lifted Tatsurou up a little and thrust up his own hips. His cock penetrated deeper. Tatsurou was in ecstasy as Sagami pulled all the way out and then pushed all the way in.

Tatsurou could feel the hard muscle pounding into him. Being treated roughly like this felt good. His body quivered with pleasure and he was breathing in little gasps. "AAAHH! AH! AH! AH!"

Now Sagami supported Tatsurou's body. He moved his hands over Tatsurou's chest and found his hard nipples. The sharp stabbing sensation made Tatsurou bolt upright. He tried to use his stomach muscles to support his body weight. Sagami thrust in again, with perfect timing. Tatsurou felt absolutely giddy with pleasure.

Sagami increased his speed, getting more aggressive with every thrust.

"Ngh...ngh...ngh..."

Tatsurou matched Sagami's movements, one for one. He couldn't stop groaning, but he didn't even notice anymore. His insides contracted with each thrust. Each pinch on his nipples made his hips shake. To keep his body supported, he clung to Sagami's neck. "Ah...!"

Sagami's arms tensed. He was obviously about to come. He grabbed Tatsurou so tightly and pounded into him with such force, Tatsurou was worried he might break in two. He really didn't think he could take much more.

His mind soared. Just as he reached supreme oblivion, he felt Sagami spurt inside him. Tatsurou's body shook violently. All of his strength left him as he slumped over Sagami.

"Ah...ngh...mmmmm..."

His still-hard penis twitched a little. Sagami's penis was also still pulsating inside him. Feeling this sensation, Tatsurou moaned. He was completely full of Sagami's come. When Sagami finally pulled out, Tatsurou felt some come dribble down his thigh.

"Ah…no…"

While Tatsurou was still powerless to resist, Sagami had gotten hard again. As he thrust his penis back inside, Tatsurou felt lost in another world.

"Ngh…ah…"

Though he just came a few minutes ago, his body obviously wanted more.

They had no intention of stopping now.

Feeling Sagami moving inside him was just too good. Tatsurou felt so far away from this earthly domain. Being penetrated like this, by the man he loved so dearly, was sweet, sexy torture.

Sagami didn't hesitate. He attacked where Tatsurou was weak, giving Tatsurou greater pleasure than he could ever have imagined.

Sagami sped up again, until Tatsurou couldn't even moan. His penis went in and out, in and out, as Tatsurou tightened and released. It was almost painful. His lips quivered. His breathing became erratic. Saliva streamed from his tortured mouth.

Suddenly his mind went blank.

As Tatsurou's body convulsed, his muscles squeezed tightly on Sagami's cock. His mind drifted far away, it was difficult to stay conscious.

He had lost all his power now. Sagami lifted him up and held him tight.

"Tatsurou…do you want to go on?" Sagami asked, panting.

Tatsurou nodded, half aware and half oblivious.

"Ngh."

He tingled all over.

As Sagami nibbled on his nipples, Tatsurou was catapulted into a whole new world of sexual fulfillment.

Holding a silver briefcase in each hand, Tatsurou stood in front of the Lovely Kantou branch manager's office.

The door was slightly open, so Tatsurou could hear voices from inside.

"Evidently the president of Heart System fled in the night. We'll never be able to collect the money they owe us now."

It's him.

The wrinkled old executive who had called Tatsurou Yakuza scum that day. Quite a few people were gathered in the manager's office today.

"It'll be fine. I asked one of my best men to deal with it. I expect the money to be here soon," Sagami was saying.

It was the perfect time for a dramatic entrance. Right on cue, Tatsurou flung the door open with a big smile on his face.

Today, he wore a high-collared jet black suit with a white silk scarf. He definitely didn't look like your average office worker.

But this is who I am. Anything else wouldn't be me.

Tatsurou walked straight to Sagami's desk and set down the shiny silver cases.

"Heart System's debt. Three hundred million," he announced with flourish.

Three hundred million in cash was actually pretty heavy. One million in 10,000 and 1,000 yen bills weighed about 10 kilograms, making three hundred million about 30 kilograms. The two cases together seemed to weigh a ton.

Tatsurou opened each case on the desk, giving everyone in the room a good look—100% cash, still bound up in the bank wrappers.

The executives mumbled to each other. They were used to dealing with large sums, but no one had ever seen this much money all at once.

Tatsurou just gazed at the men, challenging them to say something.

Hachi had managed to get two hundred million from Kobayakawa, though Kobayakawa had lied at first about how much money had been taken from Heart System. Tatsurou had had to go back again to get the rest.

"Thank you." Sagami nodded, turning his attention to the executives. "We have a most excellent employee here, gentlemen. Can you believe he collected this much money? What do you have to say now?"

"Uh, we were just concerned for the company's reputation," an executive stuttered.

Sagami laughed and rested his face on his hands. Tatsurou thought it made him look even more brilliant than usual.

"I'm setting up a debt collection department," Sagami said seriously. "High finance and debt collection go hand-in-hand. Until now, we've outsourced our collection needs. We have been locked into working with the gangs."

Sagami's gaze was sharp as he outlined his plans.

"But it's true, our company's image is important. We must make our ties with the criminal world less visible. That's why we need our own debt collection department. Debt collection is perfectly legal, according to Japanese law. We will strictly follow every regulation. And we have the right person here already. He is clever and resourceful, capable of collecting money in creative ways. He also knows the Yakuza inside and out. I think he's the best person for the job by far."

Sagami's assured tone of voice explained how it would be, leaving absolutely no room for complaint. Even the executives seemed satisfied. The persuasive power of three hundred million was enormous.

Does he mean I'll be in charge?

Sagami sent the executives away, leaving him alone with Tatsurou. As soon as the door was closed, Sagami burst into roaring laughter.

"What do you think?" he managed to ask. "Will you supervise my new department?"

"I…I guess so…" Tatsurou stuttered.

Can I really learn to collect money legally? he wondered.

He had such a quick temper. Maybe he'd just make trouble for Sagami. Then again, maybe not. In the past, he'd been involved with people who didn't follow the law in the first place. What had made his job difficult in the Hinodegumi was the need to discard his morals. Maybe working within the law would make his life a whole lot easier.

"I've been thinking about it for a while now. You'll make an excellent employee," Sagami assured him. "I had already given up on this money, but you still collected it for me. By the way, we're all square now." He reached into one of the cases. "I always give you five percent of what you collect. How much is five percent of three hundred million?"

After working it out in his head, Tatsurou couldn't believe it would be okay to take that much money.

"Fifteen million," he answered.

"I'll subtract the money you still owe me from that," Sagami said briskly.

He wasn't even going to bargain, he would just give Tatsurou the money, no questions asked. He quickly counted out fifteen million. "This is yours."

"You're kidding, right?" Tatsurou gaped.

"That was my promise," Sagami said firmly.

"I'll give some to Hachi," Tatsurou said.

Because of Hachi, they had been able to easily manipulate Kobayakawa, which gained them more respect with the other Yakuza in the city. Tatsurou expected no more trouble from the gangs when he had to collect money. Hell, he just might be able to manage the work Sagami so desperately wanted to give him.

"So this has wiped out my loan?" he asked.

"Of course." Sagami opened a safe at the end of the room and took out a document. "You still owe me four million. I'll take that from your share." He counted the bills with grand, purposeful movements. He put the contract and the remaining money in the middle of the

desk, then pushed it towards Tatsurou. "You borrowed eight million, now you've paid it all off."

"Does this mean my body's my own again?" Tatsurou asked.

Suddenly he picked up the contract and tore it to shreds, then tossed them into the air like confetti. They floated down like snowflakes. He no longer had a loan on his body, but almost felt sad about it.

"I would still like you to come and work for me," Sagami said.

Tatsurou loved being near Sagami, and had already made up his mind. But instead of saying yes, he nodded vaguely.

"I'll think about it," he said.

"Now that there's no more loan, are we still a couple?" Sagami asked softly.

Tatsurou's pulse sped up when he heard Sagami's voice change its tone.

"Wha-what…" he stuttered.

"Well?" Sagami prompted.

Tatsurou just stared at Sagami. He really didn't care for the question, since they'd already showed how much they cared for each other.

"You…!" Tatsurou scrunched up the stack of bills in his hand and threw them back at Sagami. The wrapping fell off, scattering bills across the room.

Tatsurou climbed onto the desk and grabbed Sagami's tie. He yanked Sagami towards him, and kissed his lover firmly on the lips.

"Mmmmm…ngh."

It was a deep and passionate kiss. Before,

Sagami had dominated all their kisses. Whenever it seemed like they would stop, they just changed angles. Tatsurou closed his eyes and lost himself in the sensation. Sagami's warm breath filled his mouth. All of these feelings excited him. He wanted to give his entire self to this man.

"I won't let this be the end," he promised, as the bills fluttered around them.

Sagami smiled sweetly, wrapped his arms around Tatsurou's waist and pulled him in.

Tatsurou got down from the desk and straddled Sagami.

He got goosebumps as Sagami's hand roamed inside his clothes, seeking his naked flesh.

"That's what I wanted you to say. I never want you to leave me," Sagami said, smiling mischievously.

Did I ever even have a choice? Tatsurou wondered.

It appeared that Sagami had deceived him from the start. Everything had turned out just as Sagami wanted.

"You're getting excited," Sagami said, stealing another kiss.

The time for doubting was over.

Tatsurou's defenses finally crumbled and he lost himself in the sweet embrace.

END

Afterword

Thank you so much for picking up "Sleeping with Money."

I wanted to write a story about a Yakuza who gets slapped in the face with bills and is told, "If you want money, then do what I say."

I also wanted to make it exciting. I worked hard to give it romance, a good plot, and all the things a girl dreams of. That's what I aimed for, anyway. I went to my editor and said, "Every girl dreams of slapping a guy in the face while drinking brandy." My editor said they didn't. So maybe it's not every girl's dream, just Oi-chan's dream?

Oi-chan is currently obsessed with a 52-year-old manager, and wants to do bad things to him. She tells her friends, "He smells like flowers. Like roses." But they all tell her it's just old-man smell. No one understands her, everyone just pities her. But you can feel deep emotion at any age. She's so much in love, his old-man smell smells like flowers to her!

But old-man smell has nothing to do with my story! All the men in here are handsome 20-somethings! I promise! It sounds kind of sketchy, but I promise you! Don't believe me? You'll just have to buy the book and find out for yourself… (bows)

Anyway, a stubborn Yakuza finds himself tied up and his body used, but he learns to enjoy it. I thought that its first magazine publication would be the end of it, but it received such a good reception, my editor asked me to make it into a novel.

I was so happy! I took a sip of brandy and wondered how a Yakuza could be used next! That's a lie. There was no brandy. It was shochu. I put some in my tea cup and drank it while I worked out the plot. I was so excited because my editor phoned me. I was looking forward to writing about a kid that had chosen the wrong path in life. It was paradise.

Saya Fujii kindly drew the pictures of my fantasy world. I'm so grateful. She really made Tatsurou look wonderful in his white suit. When I was writing the novel, I kept the illustrations by my side to inspire me. I really want to thank her.

Also, kudos to my always-enthusiastic editor. My editor has always been an amazing help, full of great advice. I want to offer my gratitude. I'm always getting carried away by my enthusiasm, then asking her for help to make things look better. My editor always helps me find the bits that don't work and gets them to flow into the story. I'm always astonished at how right my editor is, and sometimes wince at my own work. I asked my editor if it was okay for me to use them in my afterword, but my editor got all flustered. After muttering, "I wish there had been a picture of Hachi…," my editor then said "Do as you wish, I don't mind." (laughs)

Well, I wanted to make this interesting, but managed to write an afterword that talked about old-man smell. Thank you to everyone who reads this! Please send me your feedback!

BRINGING NEW MEANING TO THE WORD
ANDROGYNY

A Novel

Written By: Kyoko Akitsu

Illustrated By: Tooko Miyagi

Creator of
Il gatto sul G.

A Promise of Romance

契約―ブランドロマンス

Available Now!

ISBN: 978-1-56970-710-4

$8.95

TAIYOH TOSHO

June

www.bs-garden.com | junemanga.com

Every Boss Needs A HARD worker

CAGED SLAVE
密室の虜
A Novel

Available Now!

Written by Yuiko Takamura
Illustrated by An Kanae

ISBN:#978-156970-735-7 $8.95

OAKLA PUBLISHING
www.oakla.com

june
junemanga.com

IN SPACE, NO ONE CAN HEAR YOU... MOAN?

Ai No Kusabi 間の楔
The Space Between
Vol. 1
STRANGER

A novel
Written and illustrated
by Rieko Yoshihara

Vol. 1: Stranger   ISBN: 978-1-56970-782-1 $8.95
Vol. 2: Destiny   ISBN: 978-1-56970-783-8 $8.95
Vol. 3: Nightmare   ISBN: 978-1-56970-784-5 $8.95
Vol. 4: Suggestion   ISBN: 978-1-56970-785-2 $8.95
Vol. 5: Darkness   ISBN: 978-1-56970-786-9 $8.95

Volume 1
On Sale Now!

june

junemanga.com

Less talk...

More sex!

Body Language

カラダでわかる恋心

Available Now!

A NOVEL

WRITTEN BY AKI MORIMOTO. ILLUSTRATED BY TSUBAKI ENOMOTO

ISBN# 978-1-56970-767-8 $8.95

ONLY THE RING FINGER KNOWS

その指だけが知っている

Two Rings, One Love

The all time best selling yaoi manga returns as a novel!

Volume 1: The Lonely Ring Finger	ISBN: 1-56970-904-1	$8.95
Volume 2: The Left Hand Dreams of Him	ISBN: 1-56970-885-1	$8.95
Volume 3: The Ring Finger Falls Silent	ISBN: 1-56970-884-3	$8.95

New Novel Series!

by
Satoru Kannagi
Hotaru Odagiri

june
junemanga.com

Love with more sugar coating

Sweet Admiration

其やかな
崇拝

written by Yuuki Kousaka

illustrated by Midori Shena

• a novel

Available Now!

ISBN# 978-1-56970-732-6 $8.95

OAKLA PUBLISHING
www.oakla.com

June
junemanga.com

Get Wet!

Selfish
Mr. Mermaid

by Nabako Kamo

ISBN# 978-1-56970-727-2

june

Shades of Passion

the COLOR of LOVE
コイノイロ

by Kiyo Uyeda

Available Now!

ISBN#978-1-56970-746-3 $12.95

TAIYOH TOSHO

www.taiyoh-pub.co.jp

junemanga.cc

got anime?

register now at www.anime-expo.org

exhibits
guests
concerts
screenings
dances
and much more!

L.A. CONVENTION CENTER
ANIMEEXPO. **AX 2008**
JULY 3-6